S0-BAA-267

The Wild Ways

MYSTERY OF THE HANGING TOWER

SCOTT COUNTY LIBRARY
SHAKOPEE, MN 55379

Dale A. Swanson

The Wild Ways

Copyright © 2015 by Dale A. Swanson

All rights reserved. No part of this book may be reproduced or transmitted in any form or by any means without written permission of the author.

ISBN: 978-0-9863267-0-7

Acknowledgements

This book would not have been written without the understanding and support of my wife, Diane, whose invaluable insight and spot-on critique helped me stay the course. Thank you also to my friends who served as readers and coaches to enhance the finished product.

My thanks go out to Andrea DaVinci Braun for her beautiful cover Illustration and design, and the finished interior artwork. http://andreadavinci.blogspot.com/

Thanks also to Heidi Haugen for breaking ground on the artistic renderings within the manuscript. https://www.facebook.com/pages/Pheasant-Ridge-Art-Enterprises-OwnerArtist-Heidi-Haugen/442878582435483

Once again, thank you, Jenny Quinlan http://historicaleditorial.blogspot.com/ for your wonderful editing on this labor of love.

List Of Major Animal Characters

Archie: The gopher

Chatter: The gray squirrel

Darling: The cottontail rabbit and community leader

Knothead: The woodchuck

Old Blue: The blue jay

Ring: The raccoon – Island Historian and Teller

Tambo: The crow

Spark: The chipmunk

Table of Contents

All things bright and beautiful,
All creatures great and small,
All things wise and wonderful,
The Lord God made them all.

Cecil Frances Alexander

Prelude

Early on an August morning in 1492, three sailing ships, the Niña, the Pinta, and the Santa Maria, left port under the command of a man named Christopher Columbus with the intent of finding a new trade route to the Far East. At the exact moment they set sail, a child was born in the soft grass of a high meadow in a landmass that would become America.

His mother, cupping him in her gentle hands, lifted him aloft and thanked the Great Spirit for the gift. She reached for the bark vessel containing water drawn from the nearby stream and washed his tiny body. "My baby—my son. Feel the tender breeze. Hear the soft murmur of the brook. Your name shall be Wawate Ca—Gentle One." She then swaddled the baby in the supple rabbit pelt prepared for him, and with a soft melodic voice, began shaping his future. Her song was from the heart, for she was a gentle spirit with a belief that all life was precious.

It was a time when men envied the natural abilities possessed by each of the wild animals, and man came to believe he could transfer each skill to his own person through the killing of the animal. A coyote promised stealth; a fox possessed cunning; the cougar offered strength. Every animal, from the smallest to the largest, offered something that the human wanted. The result was that no animal was safe from the danger of being killed. Children were taught from a young age that the death of any animal would bring them power from that creature. Many animals were hunted strictly for that reason and no other.

By the time Wawate Ca turned five, his mother's influence was deeply engrained, instilling a strong dislike for killing. He became the subject of ridicule, avoided by those of his age. However, by the time he turned thirteen, he had shown ability beyond all others to unravel nature's riddles, and as he grew, so did his stature among his people as a man with extraordinary insight. They said it was because he could talk to the animals, but none really believed it.

Truth was . . . he could.

* * *

When Wawate Ca was only nine years old, a special thing happened to him as the result of a meeting held by the wild creatures. The decay in morality among men and man's cruelty toward all life forces outside their own had the animals living in fear as they lost family member after family member. To the animals, the path was clear. Unless they took action, there could be neither peace nor a future for their children.

On a day that broke with crystalline skies, the animals gathered near a small lake hidden within the heavily wooded hills. Present was a representative from every animal family inhabiting the region.

The hawk, Red Tail, had called for the conclave. As Historian and Teller, he knew things beyond memory and was the most respected individual in all the families. With that respect, came a special responsibility to the others.

"*Welcome,*" he began. "*I called this council to discuss our options for securing a future for our children. There isn't a single family that hasn't lost loved ones. I think the time has come for us to take action. We need agreement on what that action should be.*"

Strike, the female cougar, stepped forward. *"As much as I would enjoy fighting back, there are just too many of them. I'm afraid it would make matters worse."*

Whisper, the white-tailed deer, spoke from her spot at the rear of the group. *"Could we fight them at night? I know they cannot see well in the dark. It would give us a huge advantage."*

"You're crazy!" The otter named Slip made herself heard. *"We can't possibly win a fight with these killers. Our only chance is to move to another place where they cannot follow."*

"And where would that be?" Red Tail posed the question.

"We could move toward the setting sun," Slip replied.

"And how many of us would survive the move? How long would it be before we would be, once again, overrun?" The Historian looked from face to face. *"Our only chance is to fight from the inside . . . we need to do what hasn't been done since ancient times. We need to create an ally within the humans. Our only chance is to pass the Wild Ways."*

A murmur spread throughout the gathering, and a palpable fear rippled through them.

Red Tail continued, *"Many of you have encountered the young boy, Wawate Ca. He has a gentle heart and carries a true love for Mother Earth. Those of you who have not seen him have heard of him.*

"He is as different from his people as light is different from dark. Listen to my words. Realize the power we possess. Then we can decide our future."

The knowledge had been passed to Red Tail and stretched back to the beginning of time itself, handed from one generation of Teller to the next. With this special knowledge, he talked to those present, revealing hidden things passed through the generations and known only to him.

What became clear was the danger that if Wawate Ca was not of pure heart, much evil could come from the giving of a thing they knew was the most precious possession they had. It was known as the Wild Ways, and knowledge of it was what enabled all the animals to share their thoughts with one another. They knew the rarity of a human that could accept the responsibility without thought of personal gain, and that knowledge made them afraid. Nevertheless, of all the humans they had contact with, he was accepted as the last best hope for their future and that of their children.

A discussion followed lasting well into the night, and at the conclusion of that meeting, they all agreed that Wawate Ca, a mere nine-year-old at the time, would be the first since the ancients to receive the Wild Ways. He would be given the ability to share thoughts with all creatures, learning things unknown to humans.

Few events happened in the world that were not witnessed by at least one member of the animal kingdom, thus Wawate Ca was to receive insight to many things. Natural cures for illnesses would be given to him, and he would have power over all animal families through the knowledge he would receive. The giving would be undertaken according to strict rules established over the centuries.

The decision to grant the gift, coupled with their choice of Wawate Ca as the recipient, produced results beyond their wildest dreams. Under their guidance, his influence among his people became greater and greater; his heart remained uncorrupted, and the animals flourished. The mindset of his people began to change. His wisdom, through knowledge freely given by the families, resulted in a new respect for animal life and a spiritual connection to the earth and all her bounty.

The teachings of Wawate Ca, the enlightened one, spread like fire in the wind, touching other bands, then other tribes, and eventually, all humans living in nature's bounty. They developed within their hearts a belief that all things were sacred, a life force given to all by the Great Spirit, and shameless killing became a thing of the past.

Wawate Ca was a very old man, rumored to be over one hundred years, when he died. His passing was peaceful, surrounded by those who loved him. His adopted family, countless in number, stretched the entire width of the plains to the mountains in the west and beyond. His children inhabited the trees that reached to the heavens, the skies through which they flew, the earth upon which they trod, and the dens and burrows they called home. His life had been a balance between the tribal wars of his people and the natural ebb and flow of the forces of nature. It was his spiritual connection to Mother Earth and all living things that made him special. Every family, in every forest, and on every plain, would keep his memory alive for the next four centuries. They would not—could not—forget the passing of the Wild Ways and the peace that followed.

Summer 1921

He had the face of a boxer. His eyes were sharp and clear, yet his cheeks and brows were scarred from deep cuts long healed. He had gnarled, immense hands that enveloped the oar handles, leaving no trace of the wood beneath. The index finger from his left hand was missing, and his broad wrists expanded into forearms thick and heavy. From a distance, he appeared pudgy; a person who liked his desserts a little too much; non-menacing, almost comical. In truth, he was an evil man with evil intentions. His low profile rowboat and choice of clothing blended with the surface of the water as each powerful pull of the oars propelled him closer to the small island.

The pudgy man beached the boat, jumped out, and lifted the heavy craft with ease, hiding it behind nearby bushes. He was through the front door of the cabin within seconds, leaving only disturbed beach pebbles as evidence of his passing. He joined four others waiting in the small room.

The rustic cabin was located on Crane Island, a small island in Lake Minnetonka, chosen because of its remote location. The men had begun arriving two days earlier, and their hidden boats left no evidence of their presence. A single rowboat tied to the short dock gave no indication of those within.

A man with a telescope was at the window of a strange tower house on a larger island, and he was focused on their secret meeting. In possession of the latest technology, the man at the eyepiece of the telescope was also a skilled lip reader. He operated a small printing device similar to a typewriter, which he used to record the conversation inside the cabin. Specially mounted on the telescope was a small camera. Occasionally, his fingers left the keys to snap pictures of the proceedings on the distant island.

There was another witness to the meeting on Crane Island. Unknown to the others, hiding inside a cupboard within the cabin, was a field mouse named Duffy. There on his routine search for food, he couldn't help but overhear the voices inside the room. He crept to the edge of the cupboard and peeked at the men holding the meeting. His report of this meeting would be instrumental to action that would take place thirty years in the future.

CHAPTER I

Summer 1951

Last night's downpour had quieted the floor of the big woods, and the air was heavy with the sweet smell of a hardwood forest after a rain. Dead branches swollen with water don't snap like dry ones, and the layer of wet leaves made the earth as quiet as a pillow, deadening the footsteps of the two hunters.

The gray squirrel was unusually quiet, his mouth stuffed with ash seeds he found scattered on the ground, a result of the deluge from the prior evening. His name was Chatter, as was his father's and his father's father before him. In fact, the name went back countless generations, being passed to the firstborn male of the family, as was the custom in the animal world.

The name was apt, for Chatter was known to continue a tirade long after its cause was removed. He learned early on that he had the ability to influence others with his incessant babble, mainly because he could not be ignored. Much to his pleasure, he also learned that he could outrun and outjump his brothers and sisters when moving from branch to branch. This was a skill that earned the respect of his entire family and, along with his demand to be heard, led to his election as the family's spokesman during meetings of the council.

Problem was . . . deep inside, he was a coward, and he knew it.

THWACK!

The impact of the stone kicked debris into the air. Ash seeds fell from his mouth as Chatter wheeled and streaked toward the trunk of the closest tree, airborne for the final six feet before making contact with the rough bark of the dead elm. His strong claws dug into the trunk as he scampered to the far side and raced upward to the first branch.

What the heck was that? His sides heaved as he flattened himself, trying to gain composure and figure out what had just happened.

Now, for the first time, he saw the hunters charging toward his tree.

What the heck is with those guys? They almost got me that time. His mind was a whirlwind of thoughts as he looked for an escape route. *Wouldn't ya know it . . . stuck on this little tree. Maybe if I don't move, they won't see me.*

Smack!

Small pieces of bark stung his nose, and Chatter moved. *Yikes, this is gettin' serious.* He rocketed from his hiding spot, choosing the longest, fattest branch, and ran like a bullet toward the very tip. The sound of yelling from the ground served as a reason for more speed.

Running like the wind, he raced along the outstretched branch toward the tip. Without breaking stride, he launched his body, straining to reach the safety of the adjacent tree. Instinctively, he knew his vulnerability while in the air, and he felt the marble brush the hair on his back before it slapped through the leaf and sailed into the woods. His claws dug into the lifesaving branch of the maple that was his refuge, and without a thought, he raced to the main trunk and scrambled as high as he could go.

Those dang boys! Wait till I tell the council about this one. Anxious to make the hunters' presence known to the others, he started his warning cry as he jumped from branch to branch during his mad race to Cottonwood, where the others would be waiting.

* * *

Oscar Johnson and Larry Crop crept forward, eyes fixed on the gray squirrel ahead. Just a little closer and they would have a shot. Pretty unusual to find one on the ground, and at least one of the boys intended to nail him before the squirrel even knew they were there.

Larry was the newcomer, the tough kid from the city. About the same height as Oscar, he outweighed him by twenty pounds, mostly carried on his upper torso. The Crops used to live in Minneapolis but moved to the island after his dad got a job driving a dump truck for a construction outfit over in Mound. Something had happened to Larry's mom. She wasn't dead, but she didn't live with Larry and his dad, and Oscar could never quite figure it out.

Larry was the first to fire. Pulling his slingshot bands as tight as he could, he lined the grounded squirrel up between the forks of his slingshot and let fly. The rock jettisoned from the pocket and streaked toward the target.

Oscar watched Larry's rock spit earth into the air an inch from the squirrel's rear end, causing the gray critter to jump onto the closest tree and race as far up as he could before settling onto a branch near the top.

It was a small tree, and they charged, approaching from both sides.

"Can ya see 'em, Larry?"

"Yeah, I think I can get a shot. He's just sittin' there."

Oscar waited at the ready as Larry prepared to fire a second time. He heard the snap as Larry's slingshot sent another missile toward the immobile squirrel. Oscar knew it was another miss. The squirrel shot along the branch, heading for the maple. Anticipating the leap, Oscar pulled back and released as the squirrel was in the air, tail twitching to maintain balance in flight. He fully expected his marble to be far in front of the airborne squirrel. Instead, Oscar's marble grazed the squirrel's back before popping through a leaf and rocketing farther into the woods.

"Good shot!" Larry yelled.

A twinge of guilt tugged at Oscar. Larry had talked him into taking their slingshots into the woods to go hunting, and he remembered a conversation he'd had with his mother just that morning.

"How are you and Larry getting along? I notice that you aren't spending much time by yourself like you did before he moved in. He must be a pretty good buddy."

"Yeah, he's all right. Sometimes he gets a little bossy."

"Larry's dad works a lot, and his mother isn't around for him. I think he misses her. You know what your father always says: make up your own mind about things, then do what is right."

Oscar had not responded. He knew that some of the things they did would not be all right with his parents. In fact, some of the things they did were not all right with him. Not all right at all.

That morning, when Larry wanted to go hunting, Oscar thought it was no big deal. Larry was a terrible shot, and Oscar could miss on purpose. But his near miss at the squirrel was making him reconsider that.

"Got any marbles left?" Larry's question jolted him back to the present.

Oscar felt in his front jeans pocket. He started the day with a pocket full of those multi-colored beauties, and now it was empty. His mother had bought them for him just yesterday and made him promise not to use them for ammunition. Now here he was with empty pockets and a guilty conscience.

"Aw, shoot . . . my Ma's gonna kill me." All of a sudden, it wasn't as much fun as before.

Larry perked up a little. "Just tell her ya lost 'em in a game. She'll never know the difference."

"But that's a lie. I don't tell lies, Larry."

"No, it isn't. This is a game, isn't it? Just don't tell her it was a shootin' game. She'll never find out, and ya didn't lie. Why put a wet towel on a great day like this? I'm sure glad I ain't got a mom around to boss me. I do what I please."

Oscar figured since no damage was done, there was no need to make a big deal out of it. "Yeah, this is a great day all right. Isn't this the most excitement ever?"

"Naw . . . this is nothin'. Did I ever tell ya about the time I ditched a gang in the city?" Larry looked into the branches of the surrounding trees, waiting for Oscar to answer his question.

"A gang? You ditched a gang?"

"Yeah . . . I was just walkin' the sidewalk, mindin' my own business, when I seen this shiny thing by the curb. When I went to see what it was, it turned out to be a dime."

Oscar was impressed. "Ya found a dime? Most I ever found was three pennies outside the penny pitch game at the Firemen's Field Days."

"Yeah, I used to find money all the time." Larry was warming to the story. "I grabbed it and went across the street to Lindstrom's and bought me a two-scoop ice cream cone. I was just walkin' along, lickin' ice cream and mindin' my own business, when I noticed four guys followin' me."

"Wow, do ya think they wanted your ice cream?"

"No—they wanted my smile—of course they wanted the ice cream."

Oscar ignored the sarcasm. "What'd ya do?"

"Well, I walked along real casual like till I turned onto Oliver Avenue, then I turned on the jets and ran to a hole in the fence I knew about, squeezed through, and was gone before they even came to the corner. I'll bet they're still tryin' to figure it out. Stuff like that used to happen all the time in my old neighborhood." Larry was puffing up with self-importance.

"We had a robber get killed over on Enchanted Island." Oscar couldn't help himself; he couldn't let Larry's bluster carry the day without a story of his own.

"I don't believe it."

"I'm not lyin'."

"No kiddin'? A real, honest-to-gosh robber?"

"Yes, sir. There's a funny-looking house we call the hanging tower. The robber hung the owner of the house in the tower before the cops killed him in a shootout."

"Are you serious? He murdered the owner?"

"Yeah. Everybody figures the crook was looking for a good place to hide his loot from a bunch of robberies when the owner caught him in the act. Fact is . . . they claim the robber hid his treasure before the cops got him. No one ever found any money, but one other thing is still a mystery. They found a chain attached to a little can. Dad called it a film canister, and it was hangin' on a branch in a tree not far from where he got killed."

"What'd that have to do with the robber?"

"It was brand new, so they knew it couldn't have been there long. They figured it had somethin' to do with the robber. Dad says that's a real mystery for sure. He took me out there last year. I know all about it."

"How far to Enchanted Island?"

"Shoot . . . it's an easy walk if we pack a lunch."

Larry bubbled with enthusiasm. "When do we go?"

CHAPTER 2

The Agreement

They were gathered in the shadows of the fallen elder, Cottonwood. The tree was huge. She must have been two hundred years old when she succumbed to the combination of accumulated snow on her broad branches and the strong winds of two winters ago. She had lived a full life. Two hundred years earlier, the human, White Eagle, was born beneath her branches and grew up in her shadow. She had seen him mature into the leader of the Native tribe controlling the lands around the lake before the white man arrived. His tribe had traveled here often during the short summers of Minnesota.

Cottonwood grew alongside the main trail and had heard the children laugh as they moved beneath her branches. She had also seen the tribe bury their dead in the woods. Finally, she had seen the Native people leave the island for good.

Her massive trunk was now home to no less than seven different animal families, and the protection she afforded them made her the unanimous choice of all the wild creatures living in the woods. It was their gathering place for discussing important issues. They were now meeting to discuss the serious threat to their future.

Darling had evolved as the unnamed leader of the community. She was a cottontail rabbit and had lived through good times and bad. When she was young, she could outrun everyone in the woods. It wasn't her speed but her ability to dodge and twist through the undergrowth carpeting the forest floor. Only recently had she started to show signs of slowing down. Her leadership was primarily due to her ability to reason and see both sides of the issues. Her calm manner and soft voice served to comfort the others, and she had a knack for drawing the best from each of them.

As Darling sat atop the trunk of old Cottonwood, she looked over those gathered in the face of this latest crisis.

Old Blue, the noisy blue jay, was the representative for all the flying creatures inhabiting the swamps and high ground of the island. Blue had a warrior's heart and would scream about everything. Present as well were representatives for every animal family that called the island their home.

Of course, Chatter, the gray squirrel that narrowly escaped the hunters the day before, was also there representing the squirrel family, which included the grays, the reds, and the flying squirrels. Also included in his family was the chipmunk and gopher population. He intended to use this council to full advantage, his narrow escape still fresh in his mind.

Intent on raising a ruckus among the gathered families, Chatter was well into his speech.

"If we don't do something, and do it now, everyone lacking the skill to evade the humans will be history. I'm telling you, if I wasn't nimble, fast, and smart, I would be dead right now. How many of you could have escaped as I did?"

Chatter's outburst triggered the innermost thoughts of all present, some questioning their individual shortcomings on the bravery scale, some working to a frenzy from Chatter's agitated words, and some observing Chatter's personal shortcomings, wondering why he consistently questioned the qualities of others while bragging about his own behavior.

Chatter continued. *"I'm telling you, I am prepared to move deeper into the woods to avoid contact with these killers."*

On the ground in front of Darling's perch stood Ring, the aging raccoon and leader of the burrow family. His wisdom was legendary, and Darling relied on his input for important decisions. The woodchucks and the mink families were represented by him, as were the muskrats and all the larger animals living in dens or in the hollows provided by the Elder trees.

In this community, like all others, the history of time is passed from one generation to the next through "the telling." Each community of wild creatures has families that possess certain unique abilities, and these talents are used for the good of all. The most respected family in any animal community is the one with the responsibility of passing this history along. Given the title of "Teller," one specific member has the responsibility for maintaining homeland history.

Ring, the accepted Historian and Teller for the island community, had called this meeting. He was a very wise raccoon, and he seemed to see everything that took place on the island. His job was to maintain a memory of the past and use its lessons to ensure safety for the animals in the here and now. It was also his responsibility to warn all families when he saw danger. He was now telling representatives from each family about what he had seen two days earlier.

"I have seen some very disturbing things happening on our island. They are particularly disturbing because they are the same things humans have done in the past before destroying our homes."

Each of the family representatives looked to one another with mounting fear inside.

"There are men, even today, that measure the ground as they have in times past. Always when this happens, large equipment moves in and trees are cut down, the earth is torn open, and a building is erected where our ancestors once lived. They are now measuring more ground than ever before."

Ring remembered the testimony from the field mouse named Duffy given many, many years earlier, and it convinced him that all of the island's families were under siege and about to be destroyed.

"All of us here know the history associated with this island. Every member of the council has heard of the danger unleashed many years ago when the two men died in the tower house. It has become legend. A grave and real danger is now upon us."

The entire council inched toward Cottonwood.

"That which was told by our ancestors, that which we have come to regard as a storied legend, is proving to be factual. The legend of Duffy has proven to be more than legend. The boy in a picture the four men spoke of on the island is now in place and ready to start the beginning of the end. It will result in our homes being destroyed. Never since White Eagle and his people left our homeland has the danger been this great."

Ring's eyes were on fire as he met the gaze of each council member.

"Whatever was planned on Crane Island long ago is about to take place, and if we fail to learn the plan and take steps to stop it," Ring's eyes softened, "we will all die."

"We must act!" screamed Old Blue.

Darling raised her paw, silencing him.

Ring continued. "*The way I see it, we do have choices. We can fight back or we can move our families off the island, abandoning a community our ancestors handed over to us to protect and maintain for our children.*"

"*Let's fight, let's fight.*" Blue was getting warmed up.

"*Let's move to where we'll be safe.*" Chatter's fear from his brush with the two boys was still fresh in his mind.

Ring raised up on his rear legs and extended his front legs forward. "*Listen to me!*"

The animals turned again toward the raccoon.

"*We can move our families . . . but where will we go? We can fight back . . . but there is no way we can win that battle. We don't even know what we are up against. I do know that they are now measuring the entire island. We need to discover what the men planned on Crane Island before we can take steps to stop it.*"

Chatter responded, "*Well, that's just great. We don't know how or when we will be destroyed, and we can't fight back because we don't know their plan.*"

Ring spoke, "*Quiet, Chatter! There is a third choice. Just be silent and listen to Darling.*" Ring stepped back.

There was absolute silence. All eyes turned to the soft-spoken cottontail.

"*We can do what hasn't been done for over four hundred years,*" Darling began, "*we can offer the Wild Ways to a human.*"

"*Ain't happening,*" muttered Chatter, his arms folded in utter defiance.

"*As you all know . . . when we pass the Wild Ways, many things can go wrong. The question is . . . can we trust any human with this knowledge?*"

"*No, no, no,*" Chatter spoke aloud. "*If that person is bad, we will die, and we will have brought it upon ourselves. Let's just move deeper into the woods.*"

"*The woods, in all directions, will likely be destroyed.*"

There was the slow movement of heads as each animal looked at the others. Their eyes showed the fear in their hearts.

Chatter was becoming increasingly uncomfortable. There seemed to be agreement on one thing: without knowing what the humans planned, the animals were helpless to stop the destruction. The obvious answer was to enlist the help of a single human, and that was what frightened them the most.

At the exact moment the sun reached its highest point, the vote for passing the Wild Ways was called for.

It was unanimous. The Wild Ways would be passed—*if* they could select the single human that would receive this enormous gift. The last success was in the sacred hills to the west, and the Medicine Child had indeed had a pure heart. Ring knew that his name was Wawate Ca, and he had been a nine-year-old at the time. The revelation changed the boy's life, and as he grew, so grew his legend. His influence spread to the entire population, creating a strong belief in his teachings regarding the oneness of man with all living things; that was over four hundred years ago.

Perhaps a truly pure heart can only exist in a child. That was the decision they arrived at, and several families offered names for discussion. Stories were told as the behavior of the named humans was examined.

After much give and take between families, they selected ten-year-old Oscar; the choice was based on past deeds—deeds of kindness toward them—and the belief that inside this boy beat a pure and gentle heart.

Gratitude, the beautiful hognose snake serving as council representative for the snake and lizard clan, voiced her only concern. *"I am afraid of humans because they know nothing of our ways. They are dangerous and don't know anything."*

Darling's response was instantaneous. *"It's our job to change that."*

There was much to be done.

CHAPTER 3

First Contact

"Psst, Oscar. Psst, Oscar, wake up."

The voice was distant, from somewhere far away. Oscar's eyes popped open as the bright sunlight breaking through the trees and into the open window of his bedroom caused him to squint.

Oh no, I overslept, he thought. "Gimme a minute."

Today was the day they would hike to the far end of the island, cross the bridge, and explore what they now referred to as the hanging tower. Who knows, they might even find a clue to the buried treasure.

Oscar was irritated with himself for oversleeping, and he spoke to Larry, who was waiting outside his window. "How long have you been there?"

"Long enough. You said we should get an early start—not waste all morning in bed."

"Larry, give me a break. I just woke up."

Larry stepped back, surprised at the tone in Oscar's voice.

Oscar pulled on his jeans, tucked his shirt into his pants, buckled his belt, and went to the refrigerator to get the lunch his mother had packed the night before. Figuring Larry's dad wouldn't have time to make him a lunch, she made sandwiches for two and added a couple of apples. He told her they were going on a hike today, only he didn't tell her they were going to Enchanted Island, and he certainly didn't tell her about the hanging tower. Oscar's mother didn't like him to go to that place. She told him there was evil there.

He was very careful not to let the screen door slam as he stepped onto the front steps. Larry was already there, waiting to start the adventure.

As they walked down the hill on the road running in front of Oscar's house, Larry was full of questions.

"How long will it take us to get there? Will we be gone all day? I hope it doesn't rain. Do ya think it'll rain?"

One question after another; Oscar knew this would be a good day.

"It's about an hour's walk if we take the roads. We can cut off half the time if we go through the woods."

"I hope you can show me where they found the chain."

"I know the exact branch they found it on."

At the bottom of the hill below Oscar's house, they angled to the left, climbing the steep wooded embankment leading to the path that would take them directly to the far side of the island, intersecting the road about a half mile from the Enchanted Island Bridge.

Along the way, they picked up small sticks and rocks, which they threw at the various animals they saw. Had they been more observant, they would have noticed a single squirrel accompanying them on their journey, the same squirrel Oscar had almost hit the day before when he made the hurried shot.

* * *

Chatter followed the two boys as they headed across the island. When the time was just right, he would make direct contact with Oscar. He had never been so worried.

Ring had been insistent that Chatter be the one. Chatter had been insistent that he not be involved. Much to Chatter's displeasure, Ring had won the argument.

Ring had explained that first contact must come during this journey. He also explained that everything must be perfect for first contact to succeed. Until then, he must remain out of range of the rocks and sticks.

* * *

"There's the bridge." They came out of the woods to the dirt road leading to Enchanted Island.

True to Oscar's prediction, it had been about half an hour since they left Oscar's house. They had been walking with purpose as they followed first one path and then another, passing through the woods. Now with the bridge in sight, the main part of their journey was completed, and they could have a little fun.

Enchanted Island was smaller than the island Oscar and Larry lived on, and this bridge was the only way on and off the small island. A single road wound its way around the island, forming a circle. Entering from the bridge, the area to the right of the road was heavily wooded and climbed to higher ground farther away from the bridge. This higher ground dropped off sharply to lake level, requiring a climb from the lake side to reach the flat land on top. It was on this high ground that the hanging tower stood.

"There it is."

Larry looked in awe at the tower standing before them.

It was larger than he expected. It had wood siding like his dad's house, but where a normal house would have a roof, this building just kept going up. The sides angled in as they climbed until reaching a strangely slanted roof. From the road, they could see only a single window high on the wall, but Oscar knew there was another on the opposite side facing the lake. The overall appearance was of an old, decrepit wooden lighthouse built on a square base.

"Wow," said Larry, "would you look at that. Does anybody live there?"

"Naw, it's been vacant for as long as I can remember."

They approached with caution, and Larry peeked in the only window low enough for them to see into the interior without making a ladder of some kind. Inside, he saw the staircase and could picture the owner hanging on a rope tied to something higher in the tower.

Larry turned excitedly toward Oscar. "Come 'ere, look at this."

"Naw, that's all right." Oscar remained in place.

"What's wrong? You scared to look?"

"No! I'm not scared to look. I want to show you the Lookout Oak where they found the chain."

Grudgingly, Larry backed away from the building. Together, they walked to a gully. It appeared as though some giant had taken a huge stick and gouged the earth, creating a ditch connecting the swamp and lake, not quite deep enough to allow the water to run between them. From the top of the hill, the ditch widened and became deeper as it angled down the other side toward the lake. On the far side of the gully, just where it started to fall toward the lake, stood a lone oak tree.

The tree was about three feet in diameter at the base with the first branch about four feet off the ground. Other branches sprouted at what looked like even intervals every two or three feet and seemed to be almost evenly spaced around the trunk—perfect for climbing.

"How high was the chain when they found it?"

"You see that branch heading off from the main trunk?" Oscar was pointing to where there was a single large branch angled almost straight out. A short way beyond was a cluster of sticks that looked like a fan stuck into the main branch. The center stick in this cluster was broken off, leaving a short stub pointing straight into the air.

"The chain was hanging on that broken branch. Right there in the clump. Do you see the one I mean?"

Larry squinted.

"I think so."

"Let's climb up and take a closer look." Oscar placed their lunch on the ground as he reached for the lowest handhold and pulled himself up.

Larry followed.

Oscar climbed almost to the main branch holding the broken twig. With a sharp intake of air, he tightened his arms around the trunk, and his face drained of color. He stood, both feet together, hugging the tree, disbelief on his face.

There on a branch, not a foot from his nose, a gray squirrel lay flat against the bark, eyes open, no sign of movement.

Larry was almost up to where Oscar was standing, unaware of what was happening above.

Oscar, regaining his composure, looked into the eyes of the squirrel. *Is he alive? Why doesn't he move?*

Oscar stood without movement. *What is this? Look at how he stares at me.* He saw the hair on the squirrel's sides move as he breathed. He saw the nostrils widen with every breath. He was so close Oscar could almost feel the air expelled from the squirrel's lungs, and yet, neither the squirrel nor Oscar seemed to be afraid. The squirrel seemed to be trying to tell him something.

Softly, very softly, Oscar could hear a sound coming from the squirrel.

"Chik, chikka. Chik, chikkret, chik, chikkret."

Oscar, his head cocked slightly to allow him to hear better, was amazed. What he heard from the squirrel sounded like, "Keep secret, keep secret."

"What the heck's goin' on?" Larry was reaching up to grab the branch Oscar was standing on. Oscar couldn't speak; all he could do was stare at the squirrel that remained invisible from where Larry stood.

There was now silence from the squirrel, and as his eyelids blinked, the spell was broken.

"You better not come any higher. It looks like the branch is cracked," Oscar fibbed.

"That's okay, I can see it from here." Oscar was pretty sure his friend was uncomfortable climbing trees. He'd seen it before, and he felt relief knowing that Larry wouldn't come any higher. For some reason, he felt a need to keep the squirrel a secret.

"We better get down. Do ya see where they found the chain and film canister?"

"Yep, but I can't imagine the robber climbing way up here to put it in the branches. That don't make much sense."

"That's the riddle, isn't it?" They both began to descend the tree, each feeling relief, though the reason for their relief was very different. Larry just wanted to get back to the ground. Oscar wanted to get away from the squirrel.

Somehow, Oscar now knew how the chain had been placed in the tree. He knew the animals had put it there, and he knew it had been taken from the ground outside the hanging tower after falling from the top window. He knew a crow had taken it and flown to the tree, placing it on the broken twig. What he didn't know was that the crow's name was Tambo, and he would soon meet a direct descendant of this bird.

Oscar didn't have a clue as to how he knew these things, but he was sure of what happened. It just seemed to come into his brain when he looked into the eyes of the squirrel.

He now understood that what he heard from the gray squirrel was indeed, "Keep secret."

CHAPTER 4

Treasure Clue

Larry, with his feet back on solid ground, wanted nothing more than to go back to the hanging tower and explore. Maybe even go inside. With Larry's enthusiasm and energy focused on the tower, there wasn't much Oscar could do but follow.

This time they approached the tower from the lakeside on top of the hill between the tower and the lake. From where they now stood, about ten feet away from the building, they could see into the row of windows stretching across the front of the main floor. This was a scary place, and neither wanted to get any closer. Ten feet was just fine for now. The sun angled to cast its rays into the room, and they could clearly see what was inside.

The staircase was on the right near the front door off the porch. They knew there was a window in the tower, but only darkness filled the space as the staircase climbed into inky blackness.

"Man, it's completely empty."

"Yeah, there hasn't been anyone living here since the murder, and that was about a hundred years ago." The murder happened before Oscar was born, and everything that happened before then seemed like ancient history.

Unknown to the boys, the murder took place exactly thirty years before on that very day.

"Let's scout around and look for clues."

As they approached the building, Oscar's mind went back to the squirrel in the Lookout Oak. What happened? Was it possible the squirrel had actually talked to him?

"HEY, there's a chipmunk." Larry reached to his right to pick up a dead branch to throw at the small animal.

The chipmunk darted to the base of the building and scampered away from the threat, all the while making his chip-chip-chip noise.

Larry charged forward, sure he could catch the chipmunk before it reached the small stone wall on the side of the building. As Larry closed to within six feet and raised the branch to throw, suddenly, as if by magic, the small animal disappeared into thin air.

"Did ya see where he went?" Larry looked left and right.

Oscar, racing to catch up, had no idea.

The ground was bare where it met the base of the house. The wood siding came to within inches of the ground, below which stood the foundation stones cemented in place. There was no refuge for the small animal.

"That's impossible. I had him for sure." Larry couldn't believe it.

"Where the heck did he go?"

"I don't know! All I do know is that he was right here," Larry pointed to where he now stood, "and the next thing ya know, he's gone; just disappeared."

They searched along the edge of the building looking for a small hole in the ground that could be covered by leaves. They examined the area, sweeping away all leaves, sticks, and small rocks with their hands. Nothing. Dropping to his knees, Oscar began to crawl along the path the small animal had taken, searching for the escape route.

"That's the weirdest thing I ever saw. He just disappeared." Larry got to his feet and brushed the dirt off the knees of his jeans.

Oscar was examining the foundation. If he had been standing up, he would never have seen it. As it was, it was pure luck he made the discovery behind the bottom row of boards. Crawling along the foundation, he placed his hand on a small stick, which rolled with the contact. A branch protruding from the stick whipped upward into a crevice between the bottom board and the foundation of the house, and Oscar heard a click followed by a slight rattle. By laying his head on the ground and looking behind the board, he could see the loop of a small chain.

"Larry, look at this!" There was excitement in Oscar's voice. Larry dropped to the ground and positioned his head to peek behind the board. He could see it, but his fingers couldn't reach it. "I can't grab it."

"Let me give it a shot."

Larry grudgingly backed away.

Oscar was able to get his fingers on the end of the chain. He pulled gently, and it began to slide out from behind the board. He was able to expose about one inch before he could pull no more.

"I can't pull any more. I don't want to break it."

"Here, let me try." Larry elbowed into position to take the end of the chain.

"No way, let's not break it. There must be somethin' on the other end that doesn't fit through the crack. Find a branch we can pry the board with."

Larry jumped to his feet; the disappointment of not being able to pull the chain was gone as he searched for a tool to pry the board. He returned with a stick that would fit between the cement foundation and the bottom board. By placing it at an angle in the small space, he was able to pry on the board. He could feel it moving.

"It feels looser, can you pry a little harder?"

Larry pulled up on the stick with all his might. CRAACKKK! The stick broke in two pieces, and Larry fell backward, landing on his rear end in the dirt. His face turned red with embarrassment. Just at the moment the stick broke, the chain fell free and dropped from behind the board.

As Larry picked himself up and began to brush the dirt from his backside, Oscar let out a cry. There, in his hand, was a chain about twelve inches long. Attached to the other end was the reason it was stuck in the narrow crevice.

A brass key.

It was just like the key his parents used when they wanted to lock the house when they went on vacation. It had tape on it. Turning the key over, he saw on the other side there was another key held in place by friction tape. Smaller than the brass key, it looked like it was for a miniature door—or a padlock

CHAPTER 5

The Secret of the Map Room

"*You were successful.*" Blue leaned forward on his perch.

"*Yes,*" replied Chatter. "*I made contact in the Lookout Oak.*" His body shuddered when he remembered how frightened he had been when his eyes first made contact with Oscar's.

They gathered in the beech tree bordering the swamp on the opposite side of the road from the hanging tower. Tambo joined them. Tambo was the great-grandson of the crow who had picked the chain and film canister off the ground and placed it in the Lookout Oak. He now perched on a branch listening to the conversation taking place between Blue and Chatter.

"Do you think it's safe to take the next step?" Blue's query was directed toward Chatter. His concern was obvious by the tone in his voice. He had seen Chatter make contact with Oscar, and he had watched as the boys climbed down the tree and chased Spark with a stick. He had also flown back to Cottonwood to report what he witnessed to the main council. It was they who directed Blue to ask the question.

Chatter answered, *"I think, as scary as it is to be near a human, Spark was in no real danger. He knew exactly where to duck behind the bottom row of boards because he helped me make the hole years ago. Who has been selected to take Oscar to the next step?"*

Chatter's full tail bobbed and twitched with every word, and Blue sensed that the squirrel was fearful of learning about the decisions made at Cottonwood earlier in the day.

"The council thought," Blue hesitated, *"since the first contact was so successful, your family should continue to prepare Oscar for accepting the Wild Ways."* He quickly added, *"You will have help whenever you need it. Ring is on his way to this place, and it will be he who opens the invisible door in Oscar's mind to allow him to receive the Wild Ways."*

Chatter's breath caught in his throat at the news of his continued involvement. It was expected, yet it sent a chill down the length of his body. Not one of the animals now living on the island had ever passed the Wild Ways to a human.

All the animals had been taught the proper method, but Chatter knew, as did the others, that many things could go wrong. Suspecting his family would play a pivotal role in the transfer, he had earlier formed a strategy for how to proceed.

After a short pause, he said, *"I would like to have Tambo help me."*

* * *

The most critical part of passing the Wild Ways successfully was the choice of a recipient. If Oscar was not the right choice, it was already too late. Spreading the contact between two or more families increased the odds for success while at the same time expanding the danger to more animals. Chatter believed in the multiple family approach.

"I think we need to have Tambo make the next contact," stated Chatter. *"Oscar knows a crow placed the chain in the tree, so it makes sense for Tambo to direct his thoughts and create another link toward passing the Wild Ways to Oscar."*

"Not I, not I," cried Tambo, now joining in the conversation. *"I've spent my entire life avoiding humans. They're dangerous, and they've used their long guns to hunt my family. How do I know this boy won't harm me?"* Spontaneously, he screamed, *"Danger, danger . . . much danger!"* He was working himself into a frenzy, bouncing to and fro.

Chatter saw the fear in Tambo's eyes as he hopped from branch to branch, looking this way and that. "Chat, chik-chik." His tail twitched with each sound. *"You are no more afraid than I was. Make up your mind. Go now. Fly to the meeting place. Hear what Darling has to say. She will convince you."*

In a loud voice, Tambo cried, *"CAW, I go."* He spread his wings, jumped from the branch, and sailed between the nearby trees toward Cottonwood to meet with Darling and the rest of the Island Council.

Chatter knew the dangers of the next step. To create an understanding between human and animal, another contact must be made. This contact must take place before Oscar and Ring, the Teller, met. The plan was for Tambo to pass thoughts to Oscar and have Oscar use his mind to talk to a different family animal. Doing so would enhance his ability to talk to all animals after the passing of the Wild Ways.

It was Ring who decided who would assist Tambo in the two-way thought transfer with the human. Ring's choice was a striped gopher named Archie. He knew that Archie would object, but he also knew that he was the best choice. Archie was blessed with the ability to look beyond what others may think. He was task oriented, and once he started something, he always finished. In addition, Archie was always talking. His mind was always working, mostly with complaints, but nonetheless working. Ring informed Tambo with instructions to keep the choice quiet until the time was right to enlist the gopher's help.

Chatter and Blue sat in the beech tree for several minutes, each wondering what lay ahead for them. Finally, Blue hopped to the branch near where Chatter now rested.

"Where does it lead? The escape hole behind the board."

"It leads directly into the map room, and then into the main house," stated Chatter.

The "map room" was nothing more than a small wooden box nailed under the floorboards from inside the house. The creatures had referred to this area as the map room ever since the man with the spyglass pried up the board from the room and nailed the box to the support beam below. With the floorboard replaced, it was nearly impossible to tell the tiny space existed. Inside the wooden box, the man had placed a smaller metal box containing a map. On top of the metal box, he placed two keys that were taped together. A short loop of chain was run through the hole at the base of the larger key.

The wooden box the animals called the map room served as a passage into the house. The mouse family had chewed a hole in the corner, and they used the box as a hallway into the interior of the building, finally entering through a crack in the floorboard. With continued use of the path through the box, and clamoring over and around the keys, the chain eventually slipped through a crack in the bottom of the box and reached nearly to the ground, leading to Oscar's discovery.

The animals knew the map showed the location of the items the man had hidden near the house.

They also knew those items were not exactly where the map indicated.

CHAPTER 6

A Setback

"Wow! We found the keys to the treasure."

Oscar just knelt there, his mouth hanging open, looking at what he held in his hand. *Is it possible? Could these really be keys to something that holds the buried treasure?*

Larry, excitement getting the best of him, was running around in circles like a madman, arms flailing. Oscar's mind whirled. "Naw, it isn't possible. It couldn't be. It just can't BE."

"Oh, yes it can, brother!" Larry knelt next to Oscar in the shadow of the hanging tower. "Let's see it. Let me take a look at it."

Oscar handed the keys to Larry.

"Oh, wow. There's two of 'em. We struck it rich, Oscar!"

"Not hardly." Oscar's wits were just beginning to return. "What do you suppose they're for?"

"I'll bet one of them unlocks the door to this house." Larry had trouble containing himself. "Let's try it." He jumped up and raced around the corner onto the porch, heading for the front door.

"Larry, WAIT!" Oscar jumped to his feet and raced to catch up.

Just as Oscar reached the step leading to the porch, Larry inserted the key into the lock on the door.

Oscar stopped and stared. He could see Larry's shoulders lean into the key as he tried to turn it in the lock. "The darned thing won't turn." His motions were now frantic as he turned the key back and forth. "It won't open."

Oscar was frozen on the front step, unable to move.

"Larry. Stop and listen to me." Finally, Oscar's legs started to work again, and he jumped on the porch, racing to Larry's side.

Larry, ignoring Oscar's presence, gave a mighty effort to turn the key.

SNAP!

Larry withdrew his hand, holding part of the key.

"Aw, shoot." He turned and looked at Oscar. "It just broke. I barely turned it. It musta been rusted." Larry's face was flushed, and he failed to meet Oscar's gaze.

"DARN IT!" Oscar reached to snatch the broken key from Larry's hand. As Larry jerked away, the chain swung with the momentum of the sharp movement, and Oscar felt a sting on his left cheek. Looking down, he saw the second key swinging on the loop of chain. Angrily, he grabbed at the smaller key, catching the chain with his thumb. *POP!* The chain broke, and he stood holding the small key as the chain fell to the porch floor. Without thinking, Oscar stooped and picked up the chain and put it into his pocket along with the key.

"Nice move, Larry. Now what?"

"I'm sorry. I'm sorry. Aw, shoot, I'm sorry."

Oscar's anger was short lived. "Don't worry about it. We shouldn't go in there anyway. It's private property, and we could get tossed in jail if we got caught." Oscar tried to hide his disappointment.

The two boys turned and walked off the porch. If anyone had been watching, they would have thought someone had died by their slumped shoulders and shuffling gait. Larry followed Oscar to a tree standing off the corner of the building. Oscar sat down where he could lean against the tree and look at the the Hanging Tower while Larry sat on the other side.

"Now what?"

"I don't know," replied Oscar.

It was well after their normal lunchtime, and Oscar could feel more than hear his stomach growl in protest at not eating. *Where did I put the lunch?* Then he remembered leaving it at the base of the Lookout Oak; he had put it off to one side when they decided to climb the tree—the climb that had led to his meeting with the gray squirrel.

"I left our lunch by the Lookout Oak. You wait here, and I'll go get it. I'm really hungry." Oscar got to his feet and started to walk in the direction of the oak tree in the distance.

Oscar returned with the lunch and gave Larry a sandwich and an apple.

"I really don't need lunch, but as long as your mom made a sandwich for me, I might as well eat it."

Oscar unwrapped his sandwich, and they began to eat. While they sat in silence, they were both thinking about what happened with the key.

Finally, Larry spoke, "I'll bet ya the small key is for a money box the robber hid inside the tower."

"Don't you think the police would have had detectives look all over inside the building? You know they were looking for the money too. Jeez, Larry."

They leaned against the tree, each with their own thoughts, as they chewed the last bites of the sandwiches. Oscar reached into the bag and retrieved the remaining apple. As he bit into it, he saw a movement at the base of the wall near where he had first noticed the chain. It looked like a squirrel. What was it doing?

CHAPTER 7

Archie is Chosen

After Chatter had made first contact, a meeting was held at the beech tree a mile or so from the tower house. The full council had tasked Old Blue to enlist the help of very specific individuals to assist in the transfer of the Wild Ways. Blue had flown from Cottonwood to the beech tree, where he met Chatter and Tambo. Also invited were two others deemed necessary to assist in the task: Knothead, the woodchuck, and Archie, the gopher.

Knothead was chosen because he could dig a burrow in any type of terrain. Rocks? No problem. Knothead would just dig around them and move them to the surface. Roots? No problem. He would just chew through them. Sand? Gravel? It made no difference to Knothead. He figured his mission in life was to dig holes, and nothing would stand in his way. He was meticulous and deliberate in his task, often stopping and backing away to admire his progress.

Archie was another story. He had the well-earned reputation of being the island's foremost pessimist and most vocal complainer. He was selected because he could dig a burrow faster than any of the other creatures on the island, with the possible exception of Knothead.

Archie just wanted to move dirt. Almost frantic in his actions, he could move huge amounts of soil if it didn't contain rocks, roots, or buried objects.

He had a tendency to attract and hold vast amounts of dirt and mud on his outer coat. While all of his brothers and sisters spent hours cleaning themselves and each other, Archie never found the time for cleanliness.

He would often show up at family gatherings with bits of root and leaves clinging to his head, shoulders, and back. However, everything he lacked in cleanliness and good manners was more than compensated for by his ability to dig.

"*How's it going, Arch?*" asked Knothead as he shook his body to remove traces of his current burrow.

"*It's too hot. I hate it when there's no wind. A breeze cools things down. I'll probably keel over in this heat.*"

Archie had a long piece of very thin root fiber hanging from his chin, and his coat was matted and covered with earth. "*I hope this is important. I've got a beauty of a dig going, and I want to finish it today.*" There was a single leaf remnant clinging to the back of his head.

"*Chik-chikka-chik-chik, this is very important,*" replied Chatter from above.

Archie, for the first time, noticed the others. In addition to Knothead, he saw Blue, perched near Chatter, and Tambo, nervously jumping from branch to branch on a nearby tree.

This must really be important, thought Archie, recognizing the fact that Chatter was his family's representative on the Island Council.

"Well, let's get on with it before it starts to rain or something. I hate to leave a job right in the middle." Archie shook his left paw, and bits of earth dislodged, flying in all directions.

Old Blue looked at the dirty gopher with a critical eye. *"Archie, couldn't you clean up just a little before coming here?"*

"What's your problem, you old vulture?"

"We all have a problem," stated Chatter. *"And we need your help. Archie . . . you will be the first animal to understand a human thought in over four hundred years."*

"What! You must be kidding. Not me, brother. You better find another chump. I'm not going anywhere near a human, no matter what you say." Archie's small legs began to tremble as he pictured his impending death. *"Oh, sweet mother. Not me, not today, not ever."*

"Chik-chikka-chat-chat." Chatter's body bounced, and his tail twitched from side to side. Tambo, unable to contain himself, let forth a loud, *"CAW-CAW, you must, you must,"* and Old Blue, screeching loudly, bounced from foot to foot as his angry eyes locked with Archie's.

For the first time, the small gopher with the filthy coat began to realize the importance of his future role. *Well, I guess I can listen. Sweet mama, I'm gonna die.*

CHAPTER 8

Archie's Breakthrough

Tambo was filled with apprehension as he watched Archie's performance below and listened to his nonstop complaints.

"Why me? What the heck did I do to deserve this? This is probably the dumbest thing I've ever done! How I ever got talked into this is beyond me. I'll probably end up dead. Stupid-stupid-stupid, what a harebrained idea this is. I should never have agreed!"

Dirt was flying in all directions. Oscar had just noticed Archie's frantic digging at the base of the wall. As Oscar bit into the apple, Blue saw that the other boy was facing the lake and directing his full attention to the apple he held in his hand. It was time for action.

Tambo spread his wings and launched himself in the direction of the two boys. Oh, how he hoped Chatter was right. Any miscalculation in the plan would mean disaster. He swooped noiselessly to land on the ground right in front of Oscar, his crow eyes wide with excitement and fear. He began to focus his thoughts. Everything depended on his ability to communicate with Oscar. Larry, oblivious to Tambo's presence, continued to eat his lunch, his mind occupied for the moment on what he could put into his mouth next.

"*You must not talk! You must listen to me!*" Tambo had never concentrated so hard in his life, thinking the same thought without allowing anything else to enter his mind. "*You must listen.*" Strangely, it looked like Oscar was listening. Confidence growing, he hopped closer than he had ever been to a human before.

"*You must listen. You must listen. You can hear me. I know you can hear me. You have already met my friend Chatter. He said you have a good heart. You must listen.*"

His eyes were fixed on the young boy.

"*There is a map. There is a map hidden where you found the keys. You must listen to me and do exactly as I tell you.*"

Tambo hopped closer. "*The gopher named Archie is digging a large hole beneath the boards that hid the keys. Go to the hole and you will have room to reach behind the board. Retrieve the box hidden there. Inside the box is a map showing the way to something placed long ago. You must be alone. You must be alone. Do not be afraid. Do not wake your friend. You must not wake your friend.*"

Tambo was now slowly backing up. "*Your heart is pure. Do not be afraid. Your heart is pure.*"

Silently, the large bird turned and hopped into the air, spread his wings, and with two powerful flaps, was gone.

* * *

The trance was broken. Oscar looked to his left and couldn't believe his eyes. There was Larry, propped against the trunk of the tree, lost in a deep sleep. *How could the crow have known he would fall asleep? How is it possible?* Oscar turned back toward the base of the hanging tower, back to where he saw the small creature madly digging away. *Archie. The bird called him by name, Archie. The bird also called the squirrel by name, Chatter. I know that name.* Oscar's mind raced, but his body was calm. He slowly got to his feet and moved toward the little guy digging away in his hole.

Oscar thought, *What a strange little creature*, as he watched Archie darted this way and that with movements so fast little pieces of dirt flew from beneath his tiny feet. Oscar drew closer until he was almost to the edge of the hole.

* * *

Archie stuck his head out of the hole he was digging. *Sweet mother. Here he comes. Oh no. Oh no. Now what? This is where I die. Right here in this hole.* With rapid movements caused by his fear, Archie ducked beneath the edge and ran in a small circle at the bottom of the hole, only to return to the edge and peek over the side. *Still coming. Oh, sweet mother.* He darted left and right, only his head exposed to Oscar's gaze.

Archie peeked up over the side. *Yikes! He's here! Now I die. Oh, mama, oh, sweet mother, oh no. This is stupid. Why did I agree?* His sides heaved from his heavy breathing, and his body began to shake uncontrollably.

"I won't hurt you." It was the voice of the human, Oscar. Archie had heard the voice when the two boys were talking under the tree near where Larry now slept. He had heard the voice, but it had never been directed at him. What the heck was going on? The human was thinking to him, and he could understand the thoughts.

Oscar had passed the second part of his test to learn the Wild Ways.

"I won't hurt you." Archie was looking directly at the boy. Oscar's mouth was closed. He didn't say a word, yet he could be heard. Was Chatter right? Was it possible to talk to humans? Was it possible for humans to transfer their thoughts to the animals? Archie didn't wait to find out any more. As though he had jets strapped to his back, he shot from the hole and ran as

fast as he could. He had done his job. He had heard the human think, *"I won't hurt you."* He had heard it twice. Job done. Mission accomplished. Retreat!

* * *

Oscar watched the small furry animal scurry around the corner of the building, leaving small clouds of dust in his wake. *"If your heart is pure."* That's what the crow had said. Then he had said, *"Your heart is pure."*

He even repeated it, thought Oscar.

Oscar, now at the edge of the hole Archie dug, dropped to his knees and tried to peek behind the bottom board. By lying on his stomach and placing his head in the depression, he found that he could see where a hole had been chewed in one end of a wooden box nailed to a support beam under the floor. *I'll bet that's where the chain was hanging from.* Oscar's mind was racing. Working up his courage, he reached into the void, fully expecting an army of spiders to run down his arm. Probing the darkness with his fingers and using a sturdy stick, he worked to loosen an end board on the wooden box to create a gap large enough for his hand. After much effort, he was able to squeeze his fist through the newly created space. Feeling inside, he discovered something cold and metallic. After a little more probing, he knew it was a metal box. Smaller than the wooden box, he figured if he could align it perfectly, it just might fit through the opening he had just made. He twisted and turned it, moving it this way and that, when all of a sudden, it slipped through and dropped to the ground.

Oh wow! thought Oscar as he picked up the small box. There was a locked hasp holding the cover shut. *The second key! Maybe it's for this lock!* Oscar dug his hands into his pockets to find the key he had absently placed there earlier.

He pulled it from his pocket and slid it into the lock on the newfound box. A perfect fit. He carefully turned the key in the lock, and it opened smoothly. Inside was a piece of paper, neatly folded. He could hardly contain his excitement as he unfolded the paper to reveal a roughly drawn map. As he examined the map, he soon realized it led to the area of the Lookout Oak. Was the treasure that close?

CHAPTER 9

The Wild Ways

Ring had started his journey the day the plan had been formulated. Since he had no wings to fly, and since his raccoon legs were short and his body not exactly formed for speed, he traveled through the night to reach the smaller island. Once over the bridge, he followed the shoreline to the ravine. At the edge stood the Lookout Oak where he was to meet with Knothead, the woodchuck.

"I'm glad you made it," Knothead spoke as Ring approached from the direction of the lake. *"I have prepared the chamber for your meeting."*

The meeting chamber was exactly where the map would lead Oscar. Years before, a very strong storm had taken down a tree at this location. It had been weakened by the hollow that provided a home to Chatter's ancestors. They had long ago vacated the tree because they knew it was no longer safe to live there. After it fell, Chatter's ancestor found some shiny objects inside the hollow. They were different than anything they had ever found. The council then in place was informed, and a decision was made to move the objects to a new location. A new hiding place was selected, and what they regarded as a treasure was moved. Through the years, the story of the treasure was passed from one generation to the next, keeping it alive and allowing the current animal residents to know of its location.

Ring followed Knothead to the edge of a large boulder embedded in the side of the ravine. As he followed the woodchuck around the boulder, Knothead seemed to disappear into thin air. Amazed, Ring stopped and looked in all directions for his furry friend. Where had he gone?

"Psst. In here."

He approached the far edge of the boulder carefully. There, hidden from sight, was a fairly large hole in the side of the ravine. Ring had no trouble getting his round body through the hole. Once inside, he found himself in a large chamber. Not exactly a cave but definitely large enough for Oscar to enter if he crawled on his hands and knees. Knothead had done an excellent job.

"Thank you, Knothead. This is a perfect place to pass the Wild Ways to Oscar. You have done well." Ring was now thinking of his future meeting with the human. *"Please leave me now so I may prepare myself."* The woodchuck nodded and backed out of the chamber, respect for the wise raccoon making it unnecessary for him to say anything.

Ring needed to concentrate on contacting Oscar to prepare him for what was to come. He had to make Oscar aware of his presence. Ring focused on a single thought over and over until he knew he made contact.

"The treasure is yours if you want it."

* * *

The hair on the back of Oscar's neck stood on end, and goose bumps formed on his arms. *Where had that voice come from?* He spun his head to see who was speaking to him, but there was no one in sight. He was both afraid and excited at what was happening to him. He had heard a voice inside his head. It only said it once, but it was very clear. "*The treasure is yours if you want it.*"

He glanced at Larry and saw he was lying on his side near the base of the tree, still sound asleep. He knew he had to follow the map he was studying. He got to his feet and walked in the direction of the Lookout Oak, which was a prominent feature on the map. Reaching the base of the large tree, he recognized the ravine, drawn as two parallel lines, which led to the shore of the lake.

According to the map, the treasure should be near the ravine. His excitement was mounting as he walked toward the lake, looking carefully into the ditch, which he knew to be the ravine. The map showed a large tree, but which one was it? The map noted the Lookout Oak, clearly the largest tree near the ravine. It also showed three smaller trees between the Lookout Oak and another large tree marked with an *X* on the map. Oscar eyed the other side of the ravine, and he realized how difficult it was going to be to actually find the treasure. Over the years, the sides of the washed-out ditch had eroded, making it wider and deeper than when the treasure was first hidden. There were several trees littering the bottom of the ravine, having toppled as the earth was washed away from under them. *Could one of these contain the answer to the puzzle?*

He slid down the steep hill leading to the lakeshore and found himself at the mouth of the ravine. There, he climbed over the large rocks washed clean during the numerous heavy rains over the many seasons since the map was drawn. *This is impossible*, thought Oscar as he climbed over the fallen trees looking for a mark of some type. He knew he had to be careful not to twist his ankle on the branches and stones littering the base of the ravine.

With his concentration on where to place his feet, he failed to notice the boulder recessed into the side of the hill. Suddenly—he didn't know why—he stopped moving. His eyes were drawn to the large boulder jutting from the embankment to his left. Examining the surface, he could see nothing special. He took a step backward and looked again.

There, on the side just to the right of the boulder . . . it looked like a small hole.

He approached nervously, and after placing his hand on the face of the boulder, he stretched his body to look around the side. Slightly above his eye level, he saw the opening of the hole, partly covered by roots hanging in front of it. The position of the hole and the presence of the roots shielding the entrance made it invisible from any angle except when viewed from directly in front. It was much larger than it looked from a distance.

Should I go closer? With his mind racing, he couldn't help himself. He climbed up to look into the dark hole.

It looks like it leads to a cave!

"Wow!" he muttered out loud. "This could be where the treasure is hidden."

He backed away and sat on a large log resting against the ravine wall. His mind raced. He wanted to get Larry. This was way too scary to do alone. He could just call out and wake Larry. Then he would have someone to bolster his courage.

Then Oscar remembered what he had been told. *"Do not wake your friend."* The voice had said, *"Do not wake your friend."* It was then that Oscar made up his mind.

He again climbed to the entry hole, placed his foot on a root, and pulled his body partially into the hole. It looked like it opened to a larger area. Oscar hung there—half-in, half-out—for what seemed a very long time while his eyes grew accustomed to the darkness. Finally, with a great push, he clawed his way forward until his body was completely inside the opening. He could hear his heart beating in his chest. *How large is this room?* He moved to one side to allow as much light as possible to come through the opening. He lay there, allowing his eyes to examine the interior inch by inch. He knew the treasure was here. He KNEW the treasure was here.

Then Oscar noticed the creature that was huddled in the darkness. There was no more than two feet separating them. His fear at seeing the animal made him stiffen and push his back against the earth, trying to escape. His breath caught in his throat, and he felt a sickness flow through his body. He was frozen. He couldn't move, although he knew he must.

From nowhere, a thought came into his mind, "*Oscar, my name is Ring. Do not be afraid. I am your friend.*"

Oscar thought, "*What is this? What is happening to me?*"

"*We are trading thoughts, Oscar. There is no need to be afraid. It is like we are talking to each other. It is not unpleasant for me; is it unpleasant for you?*"

Oscar's fear began to subside. "*But how?*" he thought.

"*Because you are pure of heart. You are a good person, and we need your help. You have been chosen to learn the ways of the animals. We call them the Wild Ways. You will never be the same. From this day forward, as long as your heart remains pure, you will have the power to talk to the animals . . .*" After a long pause, Oscar heard, "*Would you like this knowledge?*"

His mind racing, Oscar blinked and nodded his head. He immediately began to feel tired and began to relax his tense muscles.

"*Good,*" replied Ring. "*Then I will proceed.*"

Oscar began to feel his body relax and his mind open to the thoughts. He laid his head on his outstretched arm.

Ring began, *"Many, many years ago, before there were people on the earth, the animals owned the world."* As he spoke in thoughts, his blazing eyes began to soften.

"All animals speak a single language in thoughts. No matter where they are in the world, the language is the same. This ability ensures an accurate record of all major events, stretching back hundreds and hundreds of years, no matter where they occurred."

Oscar was hearing Ring's thoughts as though they were spoken words.

"We have a special gift beyond merely sharing thoughts, a gift that allows us to actually connect our minds. What I know can be shared with others of my choosing. It is a gift given only to animals, and only animals can cause a mind to connect. I have never connected with a human, but if I can share my mind with you, I can teach you many things. Do not worry; no harm will come to you. If we connect, you will learn many things from all over the world, things we know to be true because one of us was present for every event that ever happened. I am a Teller, responsible for all of history. There are no distance restrictions to mind connections between Tellers, but there are rules that must be followed. There are thousands upon thousands of Tellers, and each of us carries this history and passes it to our replacements. We also pass it to other Tellers, if requested."

Oscar raised his head slightly and looked at the raccoon he now considered his friend. *"I trust you. Let's see if it will work."*

Ring's thoughts were instantly transferred to Oscar. It was like pouring words from a pail. The pail had been filled one spoonful at a time but was emptied as though tipped upside down. The words came together, intermixed and interwoven, yet Oscar understood everything that was passing into his mind. In the blink of an eye, Ring told him of ancient history: the Pharaohs of Egypt, a man named Jesus and his miracles, the secrets of the Roman Empire, of Hannibal and Napoleon. Ring told it, and Oscar took it all in.

In every instance, there were animals at the center of major events of the world. Their viewpoint was unlike any other.

Finally, Ring told of modern history. Oscar heard about the pilgrims and the settlement at Jamestown thirteen years before Plymouth Rock. He was told about the American Revolution and the progress of the new nation. Ring recounted the history of his ancestors and identified the last passing of the Wild Ways as the source of the Native American belief that humans must live as one with the earth and all creatures that share their world.

He told of White Eagle and the Native Indians, and their disappearance from the island. He told of the current animal inhabitants and how each functioned to help the others. The raccoon's concentration was intense.

He told of the elder, Cottonwood, and how the Island Council now used her for their meetings. He told of the families: the shrews, squirrels, birds, turtles, snakes, and all the animal families now living on the island.

Ring was exhausted. Memories flowed from his mind. As he remembered stories that had been passed down from one generation to the next, they immediately transferred to Oscar's mind. He told of the council meeting and why it was called. Finally, he told Oscar about Chatter, Old Blue, Archie, and Knothead. He told him about Spark, the chipmunk, Tambo, the crow, and all the others that helped bring him to the chamber.

"Oscar, you must use this knowledge to help all humans understand the wild creatures. You have the power to do much good."

Then he was finished.

Oscar blinked, and the trance was lifted. He looked with softness at the wise creature that had taught him so much. He reached his hand to touch the raccoon, and Ring responded by pressing his head against Oscar's palm, drawing close to his shoulder. They sat there for a long time.

"Why was I chosen?"

"You were chosen because of your good heart, Oscar. We knew you were a special human, and we thought we could trust you. The many kindnesses you showed us before your friend moved in far outweighed the bad things you did while you were with him. We have been watching. We were right."

"But . . ."

"You will now be able to talk to all the animals. You must never allow another human to know you have this power because they will not understand."

"But, Ring, I've been pretty bad lately. I even shot at Chatter." For some reason that he couldn't understand, Oscar felt as though Chatter was an old friend.

"We all know how your friend has tried to change you. It's what's deep inside that matters." Ring was as serious as he'd ever been. *"You must use this power for the good of all living things. Of all the humans, you are the only one possessing this power. The responsibilities are huge, but the rewards are larger."*

"I promise to do my best to be a good person," replied Oscar.

"We know you will. There is one more thing you should know." Ring turned to gaze directly into Oscar's eyes.

"All the animals had a voice in the debate to pass the Wild Ways to you. They were unanimous in the decision. It was our plan to draw you here to pass the Ways. We knew of the map room where you found the keys. We knew of the tin box containing the map to the treasure, and we knew you would come here."

"Is there a real treasure?" He had no sooner asked the question than he was filled with a deep understanding of his meeting with Ring. The true treasure was already his. His new ability was worth more than all the money in the world.

Ring understood.

"The map you found leads to this spot. There was once a tree above us, which had a hollow in it. The man from the tower house placed something in that hollow."

"That was the bank robber, and he was hiding the loot," answered Oscar.

"No, it was the other man. The man with the spyglass."

"The spyglass?" He didn't know anything about a spyglass. He'd heard the story about what happened in the tower house a hundred times, and there was never any mention of a spyglass.

"The man with the spyglass was there first. He was watching the small island with the cabin on it."

"What about the shootout that was in all the papers? Nobody said anything about a spyglass. Where was the tower house owner when the spy man was there?"

Rings reply was immediate. *"We thought the man with the glass was the owner. The building had been vacant until he showed up one day. There was never a shootout with police."*

Ring continued, *"After the spy man was there for several days, another man entered the house. He tried to kill the spy man but was beaten in a terrible fight, tied up, and dragged into a corner. That was when the man with the spyglass left the house and hid something in the hollow tree.*

The next day, three more men sneaked into the house, and many shots were fired. They killed the spy man and left him on the floor. Then they executed the man tied in the corner and hung him in the tower. They searched and searched the building for something, and when they heard the police sirens, they ran from the building, got in a boat, and disappeared."

"Are you sure? How can you be so sure, Ring? Everyone said the police had a shootout with the bandit. They said they killed the robber and found the building's owner hanging when they entered the house."

Ring answered, *"There was a mouse in the corner that witnessed everything that took place."*

Once again, Oscar felt knowledge entering his mind. He now understood what happened at the hanging tower. It was a far cry from what everyone thought happened. Instead of two men, there were five. Instead of the owner being hanged, it was another that was found at the end of the rope. The man everyone thought was the robber was actually the spy man, and he was not killed by the police but was already dead when detectives entered the house.

"There is one other secret. The spy man slipped a bag filled with papers through a hole in the wall before the others came to kill him. He covered the hole, and the bag is still there."

"Do you know what's in the bag?"

"We don't know what the bag contains, but it must be very important for him to hide it like he did. It may even be the reason he was shot."

Ring, knowing the confusion in Oscar's mind, sensed that the young boy had reached his limits. It was time to let him struggle with the truths he had just been told.

Before they left the small cave, Ring summoned the gopher, Archie, to join them. Archie felt no fear as he scampered to Ring's side. In his mouth was a small pin resembling a badge.

Ring explained, *"This was recovered when the man with the spyglass was fighting with the others. Take the pin that Archie has. It may help solve the puzzle. We need you to discover why the lie was told."*

Oscar reached over with his open hand, and Archie gently placed the pin in his palm. Oscar drew his hand back and recognized the item as some kind of badge, and it had something etched into its surface. Moving his body slightly to allow more light to enter the small cavern, he held it in front of his face to read the inscription.

"FBI."

Oscar's mind swirled as he retraced his path back through the ravine. While climbing over boulders and fallen trees, he began to formulate a plan. It was clear he could never tell Larry what he learned, and he was worried about how to handle that situation.

Exiting the ravine, he hurried to where he left the tin box. He grabbed it and stashed it under some leaves near a distant tree, then walked over to where Larry was. He was just waking up when Oscar approached.

"Wow, your mom sure makes a great lunch. I must have fallen asleep for a little while." Larry stretched. "I wonder what time it is." He seemed as relaxed as Oscar was on edge.

"I don't know, but I think we should head for home. It'll take us a while to get there, and I don't want to be late for supper."

"Still got the key?"

"I was hoping you wouldn't ask. When you were snoring away, I explored a little more. What a disaster."

"What do you mean 'disaster'?"

"Aw, shoot, Larry, look at my clothes. I was crawling all over the place looking for more clues. I even went back to the tree we climbed. Nothing! Not a thing."

"So, where are the keys?"

"I lost them someplace when I was looking around. Don't matter much 'cause one of them was broken anyway." Oscar held Larry's eyes. "You already took care of that for us."

"Don't blame me if the stupid key was rusty."

"You're right. I know things just happen. Don't worry about it, Larry, we shouldn't be here in the first place. I'm not mad."

As they headed for home, Oscar felt a deep satisfaction in how he had gotten around the key issue with Larry without telling him about his meeting with Ring. Larry wouldn't bring up the subject of the tower house out of guilt for breaking the key in the door. All in all, a good finish to an amazing day.

Oscar still had a problem or two to solve.

Now, home for dinner and facing Mom and Dad.

His mind was going a mile a minute.

CHAPTER 10

The Animals Decide

Ring was exhausted as he left the small chamber. He'd had no idea how much energy was required to communicate with Oscar. It was now extremely important to meet with the council as soon as possible. The passing of the Wild Ways placed a huge responsibility on the island's animal families, and they must be up to the challenge. It was his responsibility to ensure every family was aware of what lay ahead.

Ring could feel his age as he moved through the woods on his way to Cottonwood and the Island Council. The time in the cave had taken a lot out of him, and he realized that he was getting up in years. *I need to start thinking about teaching another the duties of community Teller. That means I must decide on which animal family and pick the individual to tutor. When this whole thing is over, I'll have to begin the training.*

His body felt like he had just worked the hollow of a tree, clearing the soft rotting wood of the interior to make himself a safe home. His muscles ached.

He did not cross the bridge connecting Enchanted Island to the main island, preferring to swim the channel. It was just too dangerous to walk the bridge. He had seen many others get hit by passing cars. He was not ready to accept that fate.

He passed Chester Park, sticking to the wooded area around the scattered houses. As he approached Grimm's Corner, he traveled in the dry swamp until he reached and crossed the island's perimeter road, his last major obstacle before reaching Cottonwood. The entire trip took him until dawn of the next day.

The council members were already beginning to arrive at Cottonwood when Ring met Darling near her nest.

"*Poor Ring,*" said Darling. "*You look exhausted . . . like you could collapse at any time. Poor, poor Ring.*"

"*I'll be fine with a little sleep.*"

Darling replied, "*We must now prepare everyone for what could happen next. You have done well, Ring. Are you ready to address the Island Council?*"

"*I am ready.*"

When Ring climbed to the top of Cottonwood, the council was quiet. Normally, they would be jabbering among themselves, and it could be quite a feat to make them listen. Not this morning. They knew the importance of what Ring was about to say.

"*My friends,*" Ring paused, and the council noted a deep weariness in his thoughts, "*we will soon face our biggest challenge. The Wild Ways have been passed.*"

They stood as one amid the silence of the deep woods. With the pronouncement made by the Historian, each was filled with both fear and pride at what had taken place. From their positions, each of them in turn, starting with the smallest, dipped their face gracefully to contact the earth with their nose. Such was the tradition passed to their generation. The formal recognition for the most important act they could ever perform: the passing of the Wild Ways.

"With the passing comes an awesome responsibility. We must now accept our place alongside our human allies. To live as one with the world is our goal. We must each accept personal responsibility for protecting Oscar from any danger that may threaten him."

Ring was tired, but he continued.

"Our immediate concern is to protect our home against the evil men from our ancestors' time; the men we know as visitors to Crane Island. We must help foil their plan before it destroys our homeland. We must see that Oscar is given all we know about the meeting from long ago. He must be told of the boy in the picture, the boy who is now a man and ready to act."

Ring looked toward Chatter.

"My friend . . . you and your family must maintain contact. You must follow Oscar wherever he goes. When the time is right, you need to lead him to the papers, and he must find the chained canister. They are the final clues that must be turned over to save our homeland."

Chatter nodded, knowing he would enlist his entire family to maintain contact with the young boy with the pure heart.

CHAPTER II

Oscar Seeks Help

The trip home was uneventful. As expected, it was almost time for dinner when Oscar walked in the front door. His mother had the radio on, which was normal around dinnertime. She was singing along with Patti Page and the "Tennessee Waltz."

"Well, mister, where have you been all day?" Oscar's mother asked. "Dad drove around looking for you and found neither hide nor hair. Where in the world did you boys go?"

Oscar knew she didn't approve of his going to the hanging tower. "Larry and I were exploring the woods on the way to Enchanted Island. We found a great vine swing out past Chester Park." Oscar found himself again on shaky ground. He was not used to lying to his mother, but the warning from Ring made it necessary. He had to cover for the time spent at the forbidden tower.

"Well, dinner will be ready in a little while. You better go wash your hands, and call your dad—he's downstairs in the workroom."

Washing his hands in the bathroom sink, Oscar thought of the strange happenings of the day. Was it possible it really happened?

Did I really talk to the animals? Did they really understand my thoughts?

Then he remembered the keys in his pocket. Dipping his hand to the very bottom, his fingers closed around the silver chain. As he lifted it from his pocket and the keys slid out, he heard something drop to the tile floor. Looking down, he saw the pin Archie had given him. That's when he decided he had to tell his parents what happened at the hanging tower all those years before. The tricky part would be concealing his interaction with the animals. He stuffed the items in his shirt pocket and went to get his father. As he approached the stairs to the basement, he could hear his dad's voice coming from the kitchen.

"Well . . . the offer is more than what I ever thought we could get. With that amount of money, we could live almost anyplace we wanted."

"I know, but how can we just leave this house? We've lived here since Oscar was three. It's home." She stopped talking when Oscar entered the room and took his seat at the table.

As his mother and father sat down, Oscar spoke.

"Mom, Dad, today Larry and I went to the hanging tower. I'm sorry I lied to you." He felt terrible, but he had to go on.

"I haven't been a very good person lately. I've lied and done things I know were wrong. I've been shooting my slingshot and throwing rocks at the animals and doing all sorts of bad things, and I'm really sorry, but I need your help."

Mom's eyes narrowed.

"I had a dream that turned out to be true. I'm not sure how I know, but I found something we have to tell the police about." Oscar knew he couldn't tell them about his encounter with Ring and the others. Ring was very clear that no one could know about the Wild Ways.

Oscar went on to tell them about chasing the chipmunk and how it disappeared, and how he found the chain with the keys. He told them about the metal box and the map inside. He also told them Larry didn't know about any of this because he had been asleep when everything happened.

When he studied their faces and watched their reactions, Oscar regretted some of the tall tales he used to tell. Expecting them to believe his story about a tree bending all by itself to allow room for a huge bird to fly between its branches had been a real doozie. Then there were the times he had tried to convince them he had imaginary friends.

It was really important that his parents believe what he was telling them now.

"Oscar, do you know how far-fetched this story sounds?" His mother spoke when Oscar paused. "I hope you don't expect us to believe this."

Oscar looked toward his father, who was silent. "Dad, honest, I'm telling the truth. Here, look at what I have." With that, Oscar took the folded map from his pocket and laid it on the table.

"Well, it looks like it's been wet, and it does appear to be quite old." His father unfolded the map as he spoke. Soon it was flat on the table in front of him. He looked closely at the hand-drawn sketch that seemed to show the location of the hanging tower and the ravine Oscar told them about. It also showed the water's edge and another island far out in the open lake. "What's the story with the other island?" he asked.

Oscar hadn't even noticed the other island when he looked at the map before.

"I don't know. I wonder why that's on the map of the hanging tower?" It seemed to Oscar there must be some significance for it to be included in the map.

"Well, this is all very interesting, but it hardly calls for contacting the police, Oscar."

"Look at this, Dad." Oscar pulled the keys from his shirt pocket, his fingers grasping the broken one. "This one broke when I tried to open the door."

Oscar's mother wasted no time in reacting to that bit of news.

"When you tried to open the door? What door? Don't tell us you were actually going to go into that unwelcoming house,

Oscar. After all the times we told you to stay away from it, you were actually going to go inside?" She was beginning to get a bit worked up.

"Wait, Mom, look at this other key." Oscar lifted it from the drooping chain. "This is the one I used to open the metal box hiding the map."

"You're in deep trouble, young man. First you go where you know you're not supposed to go, and then you lie to us, and then you tell us you tried to go inside that awful house." She was definitely getting worked up.

"Can I see that, Oscar?" His father was taking the news far better than his mother was. Oscar placed the chain with the keys in his father's hand.

"I suppose you forgot the metal box."

Oscar could feel his face turn red. He HAD forgotten the metal box. It was where he hid it before Larry woke up. He could tell that his father was not quite buying into the whole story. He was close, but still not there.

"Dad, if we go there, I can show you the box. I'm not lying. It's there, and I can show it to you."

"Well, even so, what makes you think we need to call the police? What can we possibly tell them as a reason for our call?" It was clear to Oscar that his father wanted to believe him.

"Dad, we need to call somebody besides the local police department."

As he spoke, he stood and reached again into his shirt pocket. "This is why we need to contact someone." With those words, he opened his hand, and the pin fell on the table in front of his father. With great care, his father picked it up and read the inscription: *FBI.* He turned it over, and in very small letters, it said:

"To David—Love, Dad."

"Don't know if this is the real thing or if it's a hoax. Either way, I'll see what I can find out."

CHAPTER 12

High-Level Help

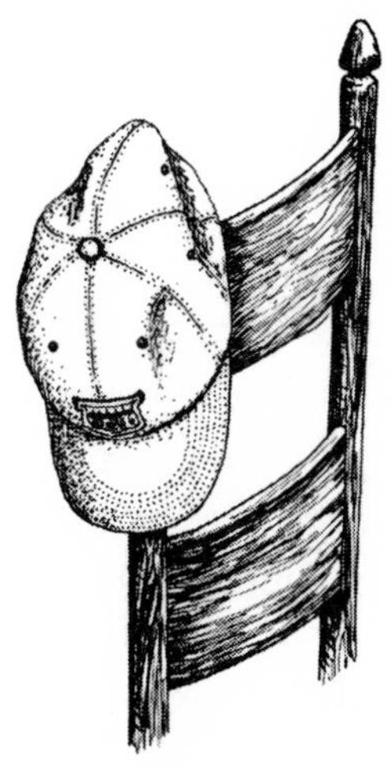

It was noon on Saturday, and Oscar's parents had gotten up later than on the weekdays. His father was in the bathroom shaving and making himself presentable for the day. He had the radio tuned to ABC to listen to a relatively new program he had grown to like. His mother had already left to go grocery shopping while Oscar and his dad stayed home to meet someone from the FBI that had agreed to meet them at their house. Through the door, Oscar heard, "Hello, Americans, it's Paul Harvey! Stand byyy for newwws!"

Oscar heard the muted buzzing from the doorbell mounted on the inside entry wall. It was supposed to have a bell sound, but Oscar's dad had done a repair job with some friction tape, so now the ring was a buzz. He ran to the door and opened it a crack.

"You must be Oscar. My name's Jim, and I'm glad to meet you. Your dad called me last night."

After a few embarrassing attempts to act like a grown-up, Oscar finally asked the man to wait while he got his father. He closed the door and ran into the hall, his tennis shoes squeaking to a halt on the wood floor outside the bathroom door.

"Dad, I think the FBI guy is at the door."

"If his name's Jim, let him in. I'll be right out. If it's him, bring him into the kitchen and ask him to have a seat at the table."

Oscar did just that, and the red-haired man followed him into the kitchen. Oscar's dad entered just as the man seated himself on one of the kitchen chairs, hanging his cap on one side of the tall back. Oscar's dad crossed the room and extended his right hand. "Jim, are you the guy I talked to?"

"Yes. Thank you for agreeing to meet me on such short notice." His manner was polished yet sounded country. Oscar figured he was a little older than his father, but he reminded Oscar of a handsome movie star, one who would exercise to stay in shape.

Oscar's dad said, "Well, I am a little surprised you thought it important enough to grab a flight to get here so soon. The coffee should be just about ready. You like it black?"

"Yessir, black as night. My father used to say black coffee stiffens the resolve."

"I've never heard that said," replied Oscar's dad. "What line of business is your father in?"

"He used to work for the government. He was the ambassador to Portugal. Well, at least that's what he told us when we moved there. You see, my mom died when I was ten. That left my brother, my dad, and me." Oscar's father handed Jim a cup of coffee, and he settled in to hear his story.

"We went to Portugal four years after she died. I was fourteen, and my older brother was seventeen. President Wilson appointed Dad to the post. Man, were we proud. We were there for two years. I went to a local school, and my brother went to a school in Switzerland. I remember my brother coming home for the summer after his second year. All of a sudden, he was a man; nothing but muscle."

"Right after my brother went back to Switzerland, Dad said we had to leave the house and couldn't take anything but the essentials. We drove all night and ended up at a tiny ocean port where we boarded a thirty-foot boat and left there just before daybreak. That was the last time I ever saw Portugal. We landed in the States four days later."

Oscar's father just looked at the man named Jim, unsure of how to respond.

"Turns out my dad worked for the government all right, just not in the capacity everyone thought. He was sent to Portugal to watch the seaport and report on ship movements. Also turns out my brother was training for special operations for the FBI and was never in school in Switzerland. Instead, he was moving throughout Turkey and the Mediterranean."

"Was your father an operative for the government?" Oscar's dad questioned.

"Yep, turns out he worked for a secret group assigned to track drug shipments into the United States. Even back then, a few high-ranking government people suspected that drugs would be a future market for organized crime."

Oscar was doing his best to follow the story while his father nodded with understanding.

"Back at the turn of the century, there were already over a quarter of a million Americans addicted to either opium, morphine, or cocaine, and a few forward thinkers were worried that if organized crime got involved, that number would grow quickly.

"Where is your dad now?"

"Well . . ." Jim looked toward Oscar. "My father was killed one day when he went to get the mail. A hit-and-run, the authorities said." Jim's voice hardened when he made the revelation. "I think it was murder."

Oscar's father leaned forward in his chair, allowing his elbows to slide toward the center of the kitchen table.

"He was very close to exposing a plot to legitimize illegal operations having to do with drugs, smuggling, and organized crime. In fact, my older brother was helping him. Their work was almost complete when my dad was run down."

Oscar listened in awe.

"Two weeks after my father was killed, my brother was found dead. There were unusual circumstances pointing to his involvement in illegal activities. The official word was circulated that both my father and brother were involved with the Genna crime family in Chicago and were caught in the middle of a turf war between rival gangs. There were even some that believed they were dealers in opium and cocaine in the early drug trade."

There was silence as the agent paused to sip his coffee.

"I think my father and brother were killed because they were getting too close to a very large truth. I've been looking for a way to prove it for nearly thirty years."

Oscar's dad asked, "What was your father's name? I may have read about it in the papers."

"Dad's death wasn't reported beyond a simple obituary in the hometown paper, and my brother was mentioned in your local paper only as an unidentified man. The truth is, the government hushed it up and gave false information to the press."

The agent paused, placed the cup to his lips, and took a long pull of the dark liquid. He returned the cup to the table and looked directly at Oscar.

"My father's name was Don, and my brother's name was David. Don and David Brandt."

Oscar's mind swirled. *David, David Brandt. Of course, the FBI pin said, "To David." No wonder he came right away.*

Oscar's heart almost stopped beating.

CHAPTER 13

Revelations

"Wow, that's quite a bombshell you dropped on us." Oscar's dad was the first to regain his wits.

Jim explained. "Now you understand why I got here as fast as I could. A midnight plane out of DC is a small price to pay for something that could shed light on the murders of my father and my brother."

"Didn't you know about the hanging tower?" Oscar no sooner got the words out of his mouth than he regretted saying them. The term "hanging tower" was what the locals called the tower house, and he was sorry for the insensitivity of the question. "I . . . I . . . I'm sorry."

"No need," answered Jim Brandt, "I was in training for the FBI when it happened. They combed the place time after time and never came up with a thing. As you suspect, my brother, David, was one of the men who died in the house."

"I'm very sorry," said Oscar's dad. "What a terrible thing."

"Terrible, yes, but it happened long ago. The worst part is what the authorities came up with: a false story that the newspapers printed. The official explanation was that a felon who robbed a bank in Illinois hanged the owner of the property. The robber was later killed in a shootout with the police."

"Yes, that's exactly what was in the papers."

"Well, brace yourself, mister, because here's the truth of the story. The man hanging in the stairwell was actually an assassin, paid by the mob to kill my brother."

Oscar listened intently. He could hardly believe his ears.

"David had a safety deposit box, and he had given me the only key—just in case, was what he said. I opened that box after his death and learned that he was investigating a person from Colombia, South America. He followed a man to Artiqua, Colombia, then back to the United States. Once back in the country, that man had several meetings in different hotels with three others."

Jim raised his empty coffee mug. "Do you suppose I can get a refill?"

Oscar jumped at the chance to fill the mug.

"David was able to overhear one of the meetings in a hotel room, and he learned of their intent to create a business. They saw the potential for making millions of dollars selling drugs. They were planning to start a drug cartel and were trying to find legitimate interests they could use for laundering their future drug money.

"What does that mean—laundering money?"

Oscar's father responded, "That means they never spent the same money from the deals they made. They had to find a way to trade their money to make sure what they spent wasn't marked somehow so it could be traced back to them. At least, that's what I think it means." He looked in the direction of the FBI agent.

"That'll do for an explanation." He continued, "David followed him to Miami, where he met with a counterpart from Southeast Asia. David recognized him from his time in Turkey. He learned they were planning a high-level meeting in Minnesota."

"You mean they had the meeting in the tower house?" Oscar had to ask, thankful he remembered to use the more sensitive "tower house" in his question.

"No. They didn't meet there. David discovered where they were going to have their meeting. He located the vacant tower house and purchased it with government funds. Added incentive for the purchase was that it could be used as a safe house in the future. You see, David knew they planned to meet on Crane Island. If you know the area, you know there is an unobstructed view of Crane Island from where the tower sits on Enchanted Island." The agent paused to sip his coffee.

"That's about all I've been able to learn about the meeting." He seemed to be weighing his words carefully. "Why they chose Crane Island and who attended it are still a mystery. David was on the verge of identifying the mastermind behind the whole scheme. We believe the top man was also at the meeting, but we have not been able to identify him or any others who may have been there.

"Somehow they learned David was in the tower and they sent a man to silence him. That's about all I know except that when the police entered the building, they found David lying in his own blood and another man hanging in the stairwell. They let the story out that David was the bank robber who killed the building's owner. What they made people believe was that the robber hung the owner and was in turn killed during a shootout." Jim seemed to be relieved to have told the story as he stared at nothing in particular.

The agent looked at Oscar. "Now could I please see the map you found?" The abruptness of the question startled Oscar.

"Uh, yeah . . . Dad, do you have it?" Oscar was a little bewildered by all he had heard.

"Yep, sure do." Oscar's father walked to the cupboard, opened it, and extracted the paper from inside and carefully spread it on the table in front of the agent.

Jim studied the map. "I remember the ravine from when I was at the scene after it happened, and I see Crane Island as well. Is the tree with an *X* where you found the badge, Oscar?" Jim asked.

Oscar, keenly aware that he must not mention the animals, anticipated the question. "Yes, sir. Well, not exactly. I mean, I think the tree with the *X* fell into the bottom of the ravine. When I was walking there, I just happened to see the round badge alongside a rock."

"Can I take a look at the badge you told me about when you called?" Jim asked Oscar's dad.

"Here it is." Oscar's father placed it on top of the map, and Jim picked it up, examining first the front side then the back. Jim placed it back on the map, reached into his pocket, and withdrew his hand. He reached out and brought his hand to rest palm up next to the pin lying on the map. He opened his fingers, and there, in the center of his hand, was an exact duplicate of what Oscar had been given by Archie. The agent turned it over, and on the back it said, "To Jim—Love, Dad."

"Now you understand why I caught the first available flight to Minneapolis."

CHAPTER 14

Larry is Turned

Larry pushed his bike up the hill to Oscar's house with an extra spring in his step. *I can't wait to tell Oscar what I've got figured out for today.* His front pockets bulged with stones he picked for slingshot ammo, and his slingshot was stuffed into his back jeans pocket, handle sticking out the top. He laid his bike on the driveway, walked to the front door, and started calling. All the kids called for their friends instead of knocking on the door. It's just how it was done.

"Oscar . . . Oscar!"

No answer. He called a few more times before Oscar opened the door.

"Hey, Oscar, I got a great idea for what we can do today. Grab your bike and we can ride out to Stubbs Bay. It'll be a great bike hike."

"I can't go, Larry. I've got to help Dad with a project. I'll tell you what: soon as I can, I'll call for you."

Larry's shoulders slumped forward, and his face showed his disappointment. "Okay. Shoot, I figured we could go out there and explore a little."

"It'll have to wait. I'll call for you when I get done with Dad."

As Oscar closed the door, Larry stood on the front steps. *Aw, shoot! Now what the heck am I gonna do?* Absentmindedly, he wandered to the back of Oscar's house where the hill fell away to the swamp behind it.

Then he remembered all the rocks he had. *I think I'll hit the swamp and work my way toward Avalon. Dad isn't around, and he probably wouldn't care anyway.*

Avalon was a lakeside park not far from Larry's house. The swamp he intended to enter went all the way to the lake. He had heard Oscar's mother warn him repeatedly to never go into the swamp because it was dangerous. It looked harmless, she had said, but there were deep pockets that were hard to see. But Larry saw nothing to fear and entered the swamp, slingshot in hand, ready to shoot a few critters.

As he walked through the chest-high grass, birds exploded from their hiding spots. In one smooth motion, Larry raised his slingshot, drew, and released, sending a rock in the direction of the birds. The miss was close, but a miss nonetheless. Now THIS was fun. He couldn't wait to tell Oscar about it and bring him into the swamp. Why . . . he could explore the swamp and know more about it than even Oscar.

He worked his way toward the center of the high grass where he saw low-growing bushes. Along the way, he fired rocks at every bird he saw. As he drew closer to the bushes, he saw they were so thick there was no way through them. Larry found it necessary to circle to his right until he was almost at the edge of the woods on the other side before he found a spot allowing room to crawl through.

Wow, this is really neat. After crawling through a gap in the bushes, he stood and found himself inside a large ring outlined by the pussy willows he had just navigated. The ground was flat with only small tufts of short grass sprouting sporadically. It was clear that he was standing in a dry pond.

Looking toward the trees marking the edge of the swamp, Larry saw the start of a small stream leaving the dry pond and entering the woods.

Now this is interesting, he thought to himself as he walked toward the narrow strip of water. That's when he first noticed the badger at the edge of the woods. Intent on chewing the tender branches of the smallest saplings, he didn't see Larry behind him.

Larry approached quietly, intent upon getting as close as possible before taking the shot. The badger was innocently sitting on his haunches, pulling the spindly saplings toward him with his front paws. He used his paws like hands, hooking his substantial claws around the main stem, pulling the small bush to where he could chew the tender branches.

At the exact instant when Larry released the rock, the badger shifted his weight and gave a mighty tug at the bush. As his body tensed, he pulled the bush, which acted to shield his body. The rock glanced off the main branch and slapped into the ground to his right. Purely by accident, he had avoided a major bruise.

Larry, face flushed with excitement, charged toward the dumbfounded badger. But with every stride, his feet sank farther and farther into the soft earth. As he approached the narrow stream, he realized he might be in trouble. He could feel the ground soften beneath his feet, but he couldn't stop running, afraid he would get stuck in the soft mud. He had to make it to the other side. Gathering himself for the jump over the water, he planted his feet and pushed down hard for the launch. What he thought was firm ground gave way, and he felt himself sinking, locking his feet in place, momentum making his body pitch forward.

Plop!

Larry found himself facedown in the narrow stream. His legs were held securely in the mud, and he pawed at the surface of the water to keep his head from going under. He knew this was serious.

He was lying in the remnants of the run the muskrat family had created to go to and from their house. Now on dry land, the house was useless, and the family had moved to a new location. The run had barely been under the surface of the water when they used it, and they had worked to dig it deeper than the areas around it. It was now the only area to hold water, and it was just deep enough that Larry couldn't touch the bottom with his hands without putting his head under the surface. He was lying facedown, body fully extended, with his arms right in the middle of the run. The more he tried to pull his legs out of the mud, the harder it was to keep his face out of the water.

"Oh, Lord, please don't let me die!" Larry whimpered aloud as he realized he was close to drowning, and there was no one around to help him.

* * *

The badger Larry had been after was named Cove. Having sprung to shelter when the rock smacked into the soft earth, he was now safely in the underbrush beyond the dry pond bed.

Now what the heck was that all about? Cove asked himself. *Some half-witted human in the swamp by himself . . . what a knucklehead.*

Cove, like all the animals on the island, was aware that the Wild Ways had been passed. He was also aware that with the passing, everything would change. He was unsure of what to do about the human in the swamp. Before the Wild Ways, he would have walked away, letting the human fend for himself. After the Wild Ways, he knew there might be some responsibility to help this human.

"*Winged brothers . . . hear me.*" Cove transferred his thoughts outside his body. "*Come here, to the dry swamp pond. We have work to do. We must save the life of a human. Hurry, he will drown very soon if we cannot help him.*"

Others in the community heard the plea and passed it along. Within moments, the entire population of the island knew of the problem at the dry swamp pond, and they responded in force.

Cove heard the "CAW-CAW" as Tambo's family streaked toward the dry pond. It would take a very large bird to do what must be done to save the human . . . or several members of Tambo's family working together.

* * *

Larry was nearing exhaustion as he struggled to keep his face out of the water. His legs were stuck firmly in the mud, and his movements only served to make his body sink deeper. He now found it necessary to turn his face to the side in order to breathe. He was pretty sure he was going to die. He couldn't continue to paddle to keep his head above water. If only he had something solid to rest his arms on.

He looked toward the woods and noticed the badger pulling on a log.

There's that darned animal, chewing a stupid log. He's so dumb he didn't even run away.

Larry was now having trouble keeping his mouth clear to take in air. Glancing in the direction of the badger, he thought, *Look at that thing.* "Bring that log over here!"

Cove nearly had the large branch free of the grass and bushes at the edge of the dry pond bed.

"I hope you guys can lift this thing. If I try to drag it out there, I will sink just like him."

"We'll take it from here, Cove." With that, three of Tambo's family dug their sharp claws into the bark and beat their wings furiously to raise the branch off the ground and carry it toward the human.

* * *

Larry was exhausted. He must be hallucinating. It almost looked like a bunch of crows were bringing him a log. As he watched, they flew inches above his head. He felt the wind from their wings, and he saw their black eyes look at him. Then he heard the splash and felt the warm water as the log landed inches from his face.

Gratefully Larry reached his arm above the water and draped it over the branch, pulling it toward him so he could rest his head on it. He was dog-tired, but he knew he had to pull himself from the mud. Pushing down on the branch, he felt it begin to sink into the mud. It wasn't enough to overcome the suction of the mud around his legs. The branch was sinking. As he rested, he wondered how he could possibly escape.

Then he saw them.

The same animal he shot the stone at was back at the edge of the woods with another branch. Off to one side, there was another and yet another badger, each pulling a branch out to the dry pond bed. As Larry watched, a pair of large black birds hopped onto the branch, flapped their wings, and flew to where he lay. This was repeated time and again until there were enough branches to allow Larry to pull his legs free and drag himself along their length, finally reaching solid ground.

He looked around. There was nothing. Not a single animal remained. Larry sat on a fallen tree at the edge of the woods. He held his head in his hands and started to cry. It was unexplainable, but the animals had saved his life. Who would believe him? He hardly believed it himself, but the branches he climbed over to escape were still there. Not since he was a baby had he cried like this. He was a tough kid, and tough kids didn't cry—at least not when anyone was around. But the animals had saved his life, and he had a new respect for theirs.

He was thankful.

He wept.

CHAPTER 15

Hidden Documents

The drive to Enchanted Island took ten minutes. Jim Brandt wanted to see the box in which Oscar found the map, and Oscar was only too happy to show him.

They approached the tower house, and Jim slowed the rental car to a stop on the edge of the gravel road directly in front of it.

They walked from the car toward the house. As they passed under the large maple tree standing between the road and the house, Oscar saw Chatter run along the roof and launch himself the ten feet to the closest branch of the maple.

"Would you look at that," Jim sounded surprised. "I haven't seen a gray squirrel jump a space that wide since I was a kid."

Oscar barely heard Jim's voice. As he ran up the slope bordering the house, he was both excited and afraid.

What if the box isn't there? What if they thought I was lying? What if I dreamed this whole thing up? His mind was going a mile a minute. He doubted himself when he rounded the corner of the building. His mouth went dry as dust when the box wasn't where he expected to see it. He looked along the bottom edge of the stone wall where he thought it would be. Nothing. He looked along the edge of the house. Still nothing. As Jim and his father rounded the building, Oscar finally remembered where he had hidden it.

"There it is!" Oscar cried as he uncovered the metal box from the leaf pile formed overnight by the swirling wind.

He walked toward the two men, holding the metal box at arm's length, as if it were an offering.

Jim Brandt pulled the small key from his pocket, inserted it into the keyhole, and turned. He applied pressure with his thumb, and the top swung upward on its spring hinges.

Although it was empty, it seemed to provide some sort of satisfaction to the man from the FBI as a smile formed at the corners of his mouth. "Well, I'll be. Isn't this intereting?"

"Look. Look here." Oscar was pointing to the hole Archie had dug near the foundation of the tower house. "This is where I found the chain. The box was right in there too." The words tumbled from his mouth. "If you lie on your side, you can see behind the bottom boards. It looks like a wooden box. The metal one was inside it. I'll bet the keys were put in when it was hidden there."

Jim approached the hole and eased his body toward the ground until he could see where Oscar had pointed. With his head in the depression created by Archie's digging, he aimed his small flashlight into the darkness beneath the building. There, he saw the small wooden box nailed in place on the floor support beam. He saw the gnaw marks at the corner of the box through which the chain had dangled, and he saw where Oscar had pried the end open enough to reach the smaller metal container inside.

He backed away and straightened. "It's pretty obvious this was placed there from inside. It's also pretty obvious that when they searched the place, they missed some strong evidence. Let's take a look, shall we?"

"But we broke the key in the lock. We'll never get in."

"If that stops us, you better call my boss and tell him to fire me." Jim was pulling something from under his belt. He approached the front door, bent over, and fiddled with the lock for a few seconds before turning and handing Oscar the end of the broken key.

"Now let's see if this thing will work the tumblers." The FBI agent used the same gadget that cleared the broken key from the lock, slid it in the lock, and turned. The door swung open . . . and Jim Brandt stepped inside the tower house.

Oscar stood to one side as his father approached the door, crossed the threshold, and followed the agent into the room. It was as though a blast of cold air was aimed directly at him, and a shiver went through Oscar's body when his father disappeared from sight. He shook it off and scrambled to join the two men inside.

The floor consisted of wide boards. The walls were pine boards nailed at an angle to the floor and ceiling. The room was bare. To the left was the stairway where the man was found hanging. Almost directly opposite their entry point was the window Larry looked through when they first came to the tower house.

Oscar shuddered.

The agent moved to the edge of the room, got on his hands and knees, and began tapping the floor with the butt end of his flashlight. As he worked his way across the boards toward the outer wall, Oscar could hear a change in the tapping sound. Jim heard it too.

"You hear that? The hollow sound tells me there is something under this floorboard. You can see where the animals chewed a small hole where the boards meet." Jim pulled a small jackknife from his pocket, inserted the blade in the chewed hole, and pried the board loose. Jim removed a three-foot section to reveal the hiding place created over thirty years ago.

"Wow!" Oscar was impressed.

Jim examined the box nailed to the support beam under the floor. "I don't see anything special about the box. It seems like an ordinary wooden box to me." The agent removed a billfold from his back pocket and opened it to reveal a small tool set. He slipped a blade into a matching handle to create a miniature pry bar. Working the bar between the box and the beam, he soon had the nail loosened, and the box was removed from under the floor.

As Agent Brandt examined the box, Oscar looked out the window. There, on the stone wall, sat the small gopher he knew as Archie.

"Oscar, bring the others to the upper room. Look inside the wall, under the window. There is paper hidden there." Oscar heard the words as clearly as if his father had spoken them.

"Can we see what's upstairs?" Oscar stood to one side, looking in his father's direction.

Agent Brandt moved to the stairs as he spoke. "I suppose there's no harm, but you better wait down here till I see if the stairs are safe." He slowly climbed the stairway leading toward the darkness of the tower. As his body disappeared from view into the shadows above, Oscar could see the round circle of light caused by the small flashlight as it scanned the area in front of the agent. The stairs were against the wall, and there was no railing. Oscar shuddered as he looked upward. When the light came to the corner, the stairs turned and continued up the other wall. He was not looking forward to climbing into that blackness.

The agent's voice echoed downward, "There's a balcony here."

Oscar saw the light move evenly across the space until it came to rest on a doorway. The agent reached for the handle, turned, and pushed inward. The door opened, and light entered the tower. Oscar and his father saw the empty walls with the stairs climbing the edges.

"You guys can come up if you want to. Be careful to stay near the wall." Jim's voice came from the room at the top.

Oscar led the way while his father followed with a firm hold on the back of Oscar's belt to steady him and make sure he wouldn't fall. They reached the balcony and entered the small room that was open to them. There was no furniture, only bare floor, bare walls with vertical pine boards, and a window looking over the lake.

Oscar stepped to the window and gazed outward.

The thoughts came to Oscar immediately.

"The small island to the left is where the meeting was held. This window allowed the man with the spyglass to see the island." Oscar knew it was Chatter who spoke to him. He was perched on the roof right above the window. Close, but out of sight of the humans.

"The man hid some things inside the wall under the window ledge. You must retrieve them. They are important." Oscar heard everything Chatter said to him but was unsure of how to tell the others. *"How can I tell them?"* he wondered.

Chatter answered almost before Oscar completed his thought.

"Tell them what you know, Oscar. Do not tell them how you know these things, but tell them what you have been told. You must tell them everything. Trust the animals, Oscar. This is the only way. Tell the man. Tell the man."

Oscar was nervous. He was unsure. "Agent Brandt, this is where your brother sat with the telescope. He was watching the island out there." Oscar pointed to Crane Island. "He saw the men that attended the meeting on that island, and before he was killed, he hid something beneath the window," Oscar blurted out what he knew before he had a chance to think about it.

Jim Brandt stared at Oscar, his mouth slightly open, his eyes registering awe at what he heard.

"How do you know that? How could you possibly know that? The meeting on the island is classified information known by only a handful of people. How do you know that, Oscar?"

"I don't know how, I just know it; it just came into my head."

Oscar's dad stood behind his son, equally amazed by what he heard.

"What's this about a telescope, Oscar?" Agent Brandt moved toward him. "We know nothing about any telescope. Why would there be a telescope, and what could have happened to it? I sure know it wasn't here when they entered the building during the investigation."

"It was removed by the men entering the tower house before the police arrived," Oscar's voice seemed to be coming from someone else. He was powerless to stop talking.

"They untied and hung the man you said was a killer. Then they questioned your brother for a long time. They beat him because he wouldn't tell them what he knew."

The tears came as Oscar's body began to shake uncontrollably.

"They finally shot him and took the telescope when they left."

His father bent and scooped him into his arms as Oscar sobbed, holding him close with tenderness and understanding until his body stopped shaking, and as the tears began to subside, he whispered, "Oscar, how do you know these things?"

It started again. Oscar felt like he was drowning as he fought for air. His father's arms cradled him gently as he cried without embarrassment. They stood that way for a long time until finally, he relaxed.

Oscar broke the silence.

"I don't know how I know it, Dad. We need to look behind the wall, under the window. There's something hidden there. Dad, I'm not imagining this. I don't know how, but I know it's true. Look behind the wall. Please."

His father placed him softly on the floor in front of him, hands on both shoulders, as Oscar regained control.

Jim Brandt moved to the window and ran his hand over the surface beneath it.

"You know, one of these boards does seem to stick out a little more than the others." His voice held a certain amount of excitement as he reached for his pocket tools. After reassembling the small pry bar, he soon loosened the board enough to get his fingers behind it. He pulled and the board came away, exposing a cavity. Inside the cavity was a canvas pouch. When the agent lifted the pouch, he saw a small machine with a keyboard behind it.

A whistle escaped his lips.

"Well, I'll be. This is a Transcribe."

"What's a Transcribe?" Oscar's dad stepped toward the agent.

"It became declassified two years ago. It was used by the agency to provide accurate recordings of conversations. I'll bet David hid it here to keep it away from the mob. Oscar, is there anything else you can tell us?"

Oscar crumbled to the floor, his mind numb, his head swirling.

CHAPTER 16

The Plot

Oscar heard his father's voice seeming to come from a long way off.

"Oscar, are you okay? C'mon, wake up, son."

It took a minute before he realized where he was. Finally opening his eyes, Oscar looked around.

His father was sitting on the bottom step in the tower house. He was holding Oscar in his arms, his head on his father's shoulder.

"Dad, what happened?"

"You fainted, Oscar. How are you feeling now?"

"I'm all right. Where's Mr. Brandt?"

"He's up in the room, looking around for anything else we might have missed."

Oscar closed his eyes, remembering what they had just found in the wall upstairs.

"How's the patient?" The agent was descending the stairs with the Transcribe and pouch in his hands.

"A little tired, but he seems to be fine. You ready to go?"

"Ready. I'd like to get someplace where I can take a good look at what we've got here."

Oscar's father stood with Oscar still in his arms and walked outside. He stepped off the porch and followed the path to where the agent's rental car was parked. A few minutes later, they were driving to Oscar's house.

"The pouch has transcribe scrolls. I can't wait to see what's on these things. It'll likely take awhile. This device changes the typed words into a coded message. I'll have to decipher it one character at a time."

"Why don't you stay with us while you do that? We've got food, an extra bed, and as much privacy as you want."

Oscar was now ready to join the conversation. "Yeah, and maybe I can help."

Jim responded, "Well, you never know what might come up. You sure I won't be a bother?"

It was done. The FBI agent—Jim Brandt—was their houseguest, and Oscar couldn't be more pleased.

* * *

They had eaten a late supper. Jim had little to say, and Oscar reasoned he was thinking of what might be on the paper scrolls. He figured his mom and dad were thinking separate thoughts about the day's activities.

Oscar's mother was washing the last of the supper dishes while Oscar was drying.

"Dad tells me you were a big help today. Care to tell me how you knew all those things?"

"I don't know, Mom. I just had that stuff come into my brain. Actually, it's kind of scary."

Oscar could see his mother was hesitant to push the subject. He supposed she didn't want to upset him; after all, he had fainted earlier.

"Well, Mr. Brandt said it could take a couple of days to figure everything out. Meanwhile, let's stay out of his way until he's done, okay?"

"Yeah, Mom. I won't bother him."

When they finished washing and drying the dishes, Oscar excused himself and went to his room. Chatter was on the ledge outside his bedroom window.

"Oscar, it's very important that you tell us everything about what you found in the tower house. We need it to solve a mystery. Something happened there long ago that will destroy our lives on this island. The man you call Jim will solve the mystery, but he needs our help."

"Gosh, Chatter, how can I know what he needs when I don't know what will happen? How can we stop something we don't even know anything about?" He got no answer.

Night fell, and Oscar had trouble going to sleep. *Gosh, I wonder what this all means. It's happening to me, and I can hardly believe it.* He finally fell into a fitful sleep.

* * *

The next morning, Oscar was up at the crack of dawn; the excitement he felt yesterday was renewed with the rising sun. The hours dragged by, and the day seemed to go on forever. Late in the afternoon, he was at the refrigerator pouring a glass of cold water

"How ya doin', partner?"

Oscar spun around to see Jim standing in the doorway. His eyes were red, and his hair was messed up. "I could use a little help if you're up to it."

"You bet."

"I'm going to clean up a little and make myself presentable. I'll be out in a minute."

Oscar heard him close the bathroom door.

No sooner had Jim entered the bathroom than Chatter invaded Oscar's thoughts. *"When you go in and talk to him, be sure to think every word you hear. I'll be on the roof, and I'll understand your thoughts."*

At that moment, Chatter felt braver than at any time in his life. *"We can do it Oscar, we can do it."*

Before Oscar could respond, Jim reappeared, and Oscar followed the agent into his room.

"This little jewel," Jim pointed to the small printing device, "transcribes each character into a coded equivalent with two separate steps. It took me all night to decode the messages on the scrolls, but I finally finished up this morning. I've got an overall idea of what they're about, but I've got the second step to do before we can read them. How would you like to translate what's left on the last scroll while I do the second step and format what I have so we can read the actual words that were typed?"

"Gosh, do you think I can do it?"

"No doubt in my mind, Oscar. It's actually pretty easy once you get the hang of it."

With that, Oscar got a crash course in how to complete the first half of the process. It made no sense to him because all he got was a series of numbers mixed together in groups of five.

Meanwhile, Agent Brandt was already finished with the first scroll. Having figured out the process, he was having no trouble making sense of the numbers. He had already filled several sheets of paper with scribbled notes, which he moved to a growing stack off to the side.

It took two hours for Oscar to complete the small portion he had left to do on the scroll he had been given.

"Whew, I'm done."

"Perfect timing, Oscar. I'm almost finished up here too. Hand me what you have, and I'll get it done."

It didn't take long before Jim had completed the entire process.

"Okay . . . you ready? We're about to find out what my brother wanted us to know. I think we have the evidence proving my father and brother were murdered."

"Wow. I gotta go tell Mom and Dad."

"Hold on, partner, not so fast. How about helping me tie up a few loose ends before we announce that?"

"You're gonna let me help some more? Wait'll I tell Larry this one."

"Oscar, you can't tell Larry. In fact, you can't tell anyone except your parents. This is dangerous business, and I'd get into a heap of trouble if my bosses knew I let you get involved. Truth is . . . I wouldn't be this far without your help. I can hardly believe what's happened, but I'd sure like you to continue helping me."

Oscar felt his face blush at the compliment.

"Here we go, Oscar. David had been collecting evidence against the gangs for a long time, and I learned that most of what he gathered was stored in a safety deposit box in a Washington, DC bank."

Oscar listened intently.

"You know the Transcribe used a continuous scroll of paper about four inches wide. What you don't know is that David's notes cover a period of three days, each day producing a scroll dated at both the beginning and the end of the data. Those records tell the whereabouts of a key and certain pass codes necessary to enter the bank in Washington and gain access to the safety deposit box."

Oscar could tell the agent was getting excited. He reached into a box on the floor next to the table and pulled out a scroll of paper.

"The first scroll is dated June 18, 1921, and contains information I already know. It records steps taken to intercept drug shipments and identifies members of the gang. This is old news. Everyone mentioned is now either dead or in prison."

Jim flipped the scroll to Oscar, which he bobbled before catching it.

Plucking another from the box, Jim continued, "This one is far more revealing. It records steps taken by Dad and David to disrupt drug shipments into the US and tells what they learned about the organization. There are names and places, most now meaningless, but nonetheless very interesting."

Oscar was ready this time when the second scroll flew his way. With one hand, he snatched it out of the air and placed it in his lap next to the first one.

Jim then lifted the third paper scroll that Oscar had just completed.

"This scroll is the one!"

He placed it on the desk near the stack of papers piled to one side.

"This is going to be interesting. When I interpreted the Transcribe notes, my concentration was on the transcription. Each word stood alone without connecting to the others. I simply wrote the translation.

"Now I can read my handwritten notes for the first time and see them as they were intended. If you have any questions pop into your head, speak up, okay?"

"Okay," answered Oscar.

Oscar listened as the agent read from his handwritten translation. As he heard Jim's words, he concentrated on thinking every one so Chatter would also understand what was said.

- ***"June 20, 1921***

- ***Today, they talk in earnest. I am ready. I have set the telescope. I will use the Transcribe to record the conversation. I have bidden the pictures and drawn a map, also hidden. I have prepared a hiding place for the Transcribe and the records. Even if I am discovered, these will be safe. It's too risky to leave this place with the evidence. I will return later to get everything that I hide . . ."***

Oscar stopped him. "He's talking about the map we found. That means there are pictures someplace. I wonder what kind of pictures they could be."

"Probably taken with a special camera setup that attaches to the telescope he was using. I've seen them in the FBI antiquities building."

"What's 'antiquities'?"

"Basically, they are things used in the past, things that are no longer in use. Let me read on, and when I hit something important, I'll read it aloud."

Jim scanned a few pages, then stopped and looked at Oscar.

"Well, these pages are pretty interesting. David identifies the men he recognized in the cabin on the smaller island we think is Crane Island."

"One of them is a guy named Carl Hendrix, a citizen of Denmark and a known past organizer for the mob."

Chatter understood every word because Oscar thought every word. With his understanding, the thoughts were transferred to Ring, who was hiding in the trees alongside Oscar's house.

"The second guy is Raul DePaulo, a ruthless enforcer, like a bully that gets his own way. He worked for a Far Eastern gang."

Oscar was concentrating as hard as he could.

"The third guy is the guy my brother followed from Colombia. His name was Carmen Viscocia. He preferred to go by the nickname Viper, and he represented the Colombian gang. He was short and round, actually pudgy looking. The index finger of his left hand was missing, the result of a mistake made years ago.

"The fourth man was a surprise to David. His name was Johnsrud Johnson, and he was a powerful lobbyist that lived in California. It was said he had the ears of half the senate."

Jim paused to allow Oscar time to process what he had just been told.

"Oscar, this makes it pretty clear that the tentacles of these gangs reached into the highest seats of power in our own government."

Jim paused for a long-drawn breath.

"That brings us to the fifth member of the group in the cabin. He was a man my brother could not identify. This is the guy I'm most interested in. David refers to him as 'Big.' Let me read the translation so you can hear David's words:

- ***"He approaches the table with his back to the window, a slight limp evidenced in his walk . . . narrow shoulders. He favors his left leg. Perhaps a polio victim? Referred to as Mr. B. Pictures should help identify him. The assassin named Olevig is now securely bound, gagged, and blindfolded, but it is just a matter of time until others are sent."***

Oscar thought, and Chatter listened.

Jim quit reading and fixed his gaze on nothing in particular as he spoke.

"The reference to the assassin proves David knew the man was a killer. It also proves David tied him up before the meeting started. Somehow he knew that others would follow the assassin, Olevig."

The agent turned to face Oscar. "This backs up what you said in the upper room. So far, everything you said was true. How'd you know that?"

"Like I said, it just came into my head."

Jim just looked at Oscar and shook his head in disbelief before returning his attention to his translation.

"It looks like the transcript changes to a recording of dialogue.

- ***"Carl: The esteemed Mr. B invited us here to provide a solution to our distribution problems.***

- ***Raul: I am more concerned with the difficulties that come with making clean money out of dirty.***

- ***Big: Allow me to tell you what's on my mind. I have a plan for solving both of those problems.***

- ***Viper: If it weren't for the contribution from my friends in Colombia, I wouldn't be here. Don't disappoint me, Mr. B."***

When Oscar heard Jim reading the translation, it was as though Jim's brother was talking directly to him. He, Oscar, knew the man with a limp referred to as "B" or "Mr. Big" was clearly the one that called the meeting. Oscar's mind began to wander as he considered the toughness of the men on Crane Island thirty years ago, and he wondered if they were all still alive.

Chatter pulled him from his thoughts. *"Oscar, pay attention, we've missed a lot of what he was reading. Somehow you have to get him to read the last part again."*

Darn it! Pay attention! Oscar thought, and then he interrupted the agent.

"Jim, I didn't understand that last part. The part right after the guy named Viper talked tough to the man with the limp."

Jim scanned the translation again then explained it to Oscar.

"I learned the basics of their scheme by reading all three scrolls. The plan offered by the man with the limp was simple but very expensive. His team of geologists had determined the bedrock beneath this island is a labyrinth of connecting tunnels and open chambers formed when the earth was young. His plan was to bring order to the passageways and create an immense underground factory for processing the various future drugs of choice for the world's users. Above this factory, on the surface, they would build the world's largest amusement park with family attractions using the latest technologies available."

He paused, leafed through the stack of papers, and pulled out two of them, which he scanned quickly. Then he continued.

"They expected the amusement park to provide sufficient capability to launder the money made on the future drug trade. It was described as forward looking with the payoff decades away. It would ensure untold wealth to the families of those who were to participate."

This time, Oscar concentrated on every single word, and Chatter shared in the knowledge.

Jim continued, "There was one final twist to the plan, and it was delivered as a warning to the quarrelsome Viper from Colombia."

Once again, the agent read from his translation.

- ***"Big: Mr. Viscocia, or Viper, or whatever you prefer to be called. Please watch your tongue. Your boss is a primary player. It will be his son that will deliver the hard-earned riches to our families. It will be his son that runs the world drug market. He will be living with me, and I will prepare him for his task."***

* * *

They were seated in the living room, and Oscar looked on as Agent Brandt spoke.

"I have proof that Dad and David were murdered, and I have proof that they were not involved with the alcohol and drug trade. I'm sure that the safety deposit box in Washington will support this and likely bring added facts to light.

"What I don't know is the identity of the man who planned the whole thing, and I don't know anything about the identity of the son.

"I need to get back to Washington to check that safety deposit box. It may shed more light on the puzzle. There's still something missing, and I need to find out what it is."

Jim rose to leave and stepped forward to shake the hand of Oscar's father. "I want to thank you for recognizing the need to call in the FBI. It means a lot for me to prove my family's honor."

He turned toward Oscar's mother, and before he could extend his hand, she wrapped her arms around him in a warm embrace. "Thank you, Agent Brandt. You are welcome in our house anytime."

Slightly embarrassed, he answered, "Mrs. Johnson, your hospitality is unmatched. I thank you so much for allowing me into your home." He then turned to Oscar.

"Young man, you are amazing. I can't thank you enough. You have a bright future. If you mind your parents and stick to your studies, you can be an outstanding agent yourself."

Oscar stood tall, embarrassed, and yet proud.

"I'll be in touch soon. I've got a few things I need to check on, but you'll be hearing from me. Thanks again."

He turned and walked out the door.

* * *

Larry woke up and knew something was wrong. He hardly ever got sick, but on this morning, he felt really bad. His dad was just leaving for work.

"Dad, I don't feel too good."

His father laid his car keys on the kitchen counter. "What's the problem?"

"I just don't feel good. I got the chills and feel bad all over."

"Let's have a look . . ." Larry stood while his dad felt his forehead. "You've got a fever. My gosh, your cheeks look like they're sunburned. I'll have to take you to the doctor. You've got some kind of rash on your neck. We're going to stop at my work on the way there. I'll have to tell them I'll be late today."

There was no conversation as the two of them drove to the closest doctor's office.

"This doesn't look look good, Mr. Crop. I'd like you to take him into the hospital so we can run a few tests that I can't do here. If I'm right, we may have to keep him there a few days while we treat him."

"So this is something serious?"

"We'll see what the tests tell us. It could be nothing at all. But if I'm not mistaken, your son has all the symptoms of scarlet fever."

Later that day, the diagnosis was indeed confirmed as scarlet fever.

"It is serious, but I think we got it in time. If left untreated, it could be bad, but we have medicine that, when used with bed rest, should lead to a complete recovery."

His father stayed with him every moment that he wasn't working. He regretted not being at home for him during the day since Larry's mom had left and they'd moved to the island, but a job was a job, and he enjoyed driving for Kraft Brothers.

Three days later, Larry came home from the hospital under strict orders to stay inside and rest. His dad headed for Oscar's house to speak with his parents.

"Poor kid was really sick. Scarlet fever isn't anything to fool around with." He was now talking to Oscar's parents in their kitchen. "Since we moved here, I've been working all day, sometimes ten- to twelve-hour days. Larry was alone, and I didn't give it much thought because he never complains."

"He seems like a pretty self-sufficient kid, I'll give you that." Oscar's dad had grown to respect Larry's independence.

"I talked to my boss, and they're going to change my schedule soon as work slows a bit. They figure before school starts up. The doctors say Larry isn't contagious anymore, and I was wondering if you'd let Oscar spend a few afternoons with him. It would really be a big help."

Oscar's parents shared a look before his mom answered. "I'll talk to Oscar. I'm sure he'll have no problem spending a few afternoons with his friend. They've become pretty close, you know."

* * *

Oscar saw a change in Larry. Now, instead of thinking up ways to do things they shouldn't do, he was interested in things Oscar was interested in.

"Larry, I gotta ask you . . . these last couple of days there seems to be something different about you, almost like it isn't you at all. You know how we used to talk about digging stuff up, and hunting with our slingshots, and bike hikes and figuring ways to do what our parents didn't want us to do?"

"Yeah, I remember. Look, Oscar, it's different now that Dad's home more than he used to be. I kinda feel bad for some of the stuff I used to do." Larry paused. "And something happened in the swamp I never told you about."

Larry told Oscar about what happened to him in the swamp. How he almost drowned and how the animals seemed to work together to save his life. He told Oscar the whole thing except the part when he cried.

"I'm telling you, Oscar, I really think they worked together to save my life."

"I don't know if I believe that or not, but I guess it's possible. I don't think I'd tell anyone else that's what you think, or they're gonna figure you're nuts."

"Yeah, I just thought I'd tell you 'cause I know you can keep a secret."

"Your secret's safe with me. Look at the new *Tom Mix* comic Mom bought me."

"Wow! How about I trade you an *Aquaman* and . . ." Larry dug through his box of comics. "Here it is. I'll trade you *Aquaman* and *Red Ryder* for *Tom Mix*."

CHAPTER 17

The Final Clue

Two weeks later, Jim was back and called for a meeting at Oscar's house. They were seated exactly as they had been before Jim left to return to Washington.

"Have you had an unsolicited offer to buy your house?" The agent came directly to the point.

"Why, yes, we have. As a matter of fact, it was nearly a month ago," Oscar's father replied.

"But it was the strangest offer I've ever heard," added his mom. "We received a letter stating an investor was interested in purchasing our property. The price being offered was nearly double what the property is worth."

Jim looked directly into her eyes. "I can tell you why you got the offer and why the investor wants your land. I would guess everyone else on the island has received similar offers." With that, Agent Brandt told them the story outlined in the Transcribe papers. When he finished, there was silence in the room.

"I am going to tell you some things that must be kept secret."

The room was absolutely quiet. Oscar's Mom and Dad nodded in agreement.

"We know the things we found in the tower house prove my father and brother were innocent of any crimes. What you didn't know was that they also exposed a plot to own this entire island and use it for illegal purposes. There is time to stop it from happening, but I'm missing critical evidence that will lead me to the top people. Without it, there is no chance of stopping them."

Oscar listened, thinking every word that the agent said. Just outside the window, Chatter heard Oscar's thoughts.

"So . . . you can see the importance of locating the film canisters containing photos of the men at the meeting. At least one of them will be a picture of the man with the limp. Thirty years ago, at the time of the murder, they found one film canister hanging on a chain in a tree near the tower house. Unfortunately, it was empty, but somewhere there is at least one roll of film hidden by my brother."

Jim exchanged looks with each person in the room. "Oscar seems to have a sixth sense about what happened at the tower house. I was hoping you would allow him to go with me. I would like to return and look for the film."

The debate was short but intense. Oscar's mother was dead set against the whole idea, but she was the only one who felt that way. Words were exchanged, tears were shed, and the decision was made to allow Oscar to accompany the FBI agent. As Jim backed out of the driveway with Oscar in the passenger seat, Oscar felt excitement building inside him.

* * *

They approached the ravine from the tower side. Although Agent Brandt led the way, it was Oscar who directed him.

Tambo was high above the two men, perched at the very tip of the large pine tree. In fact, it was the only pine tree in that section of woods. It had been struck by lightning, and a good portion of the interior was burned away. In addition, a split had been created, running nearly the length of the trunk. Into this split, the canisters had been placed.

His directive from Ring was clear. *"Lead Oscar to the canisters."*

"Oscar, listen to me. I am Tambo, and I will lead you to the canisters." He described the large pine and explained where the canisters would be. He then called out to Chatter, who lay on a branch of an adjacent tree.

"Chatter, my friend, we need your help. Buried deep within the large pine are the film canisters being sought. You must find them and bring them to where Oscar can find them. Hurry, my friend, they are drawing close."

Chatter understood his task and wasted no time. As the two humans approached the tree, Chatter exited the split and draped the chain over a fold in the bark before disappearing among the branches.

Tambo once again thought to Oscar, *"You will find the canisters hanging on the large pine. Take the man there."*

* * *

As they circled the pine tree, Oscar pointed to a spot about six feet off the ground.

"Look there, right up there." Barely exposed behind a broken branch, Oscar could make out the looped chain.

"Well, I'll be darned. Oscar . . . how in the world did you know that was there?" Jim stretched to his full height and was barely able to reach the chain. "I don't know what's going on, but I sure appreciate the help. I think you ought to be tested for psychic powers because what I've seen is amazing."

Oscar took the compliment in stride.

"It's like you talk to the animals or something. Anyway, I've got a kit in the car. Let's take a look at the film."

Oscar followed Jim to his rented car. It was the latest out of Detroit, a Hudson Hornet, and Oscar thought it was the neatest thing he'd ever ridden in. He watched the agent hastily arrange a piece of equipment for viewing the film. It allowed the roll of negatives to slide under a viewing screen where the picture was changed to the positive image.

My gosh, I didn't know stuff like this was possible. Oscar was truly impressed as he watched the images appear on a device plugged into the viewing equipment. It reminded him of what he'd seen in his *Flash Gordon* comic books.

The first roll was apparently full of test pictures showing scenes of the cabin and the shoreline, using various camera settings to get the clearest, most concise images possible. Only one picture showing a man dropping a rowboat into the bushes seemed to be of any interest to the agent.

Oscar sat patiently while Jim loaded the second roll and began to examine the film.

"Now we're talking," Jim muttered the remark, mostly to himself.

Oscar watched as the pictures showed five men seated at a table. A shade in the window hid the top half of the face of one of the men. The others were clearly visible and easily identifiable.

Scanning from picture to picture, they came to one where the man with the half-hidden face leaned forward, pointing his finger at another. His head was turned directly toward the camera.

Oscar heard a soft whistle escape the agent's lips.

"My gosh! This is dynamite! The man with the limp is none other than Congressman Bouvoir. Oscar, this is dynamite! Bouvoir has been in the House of Representatives for a long time. He serves on President Truman's committee to explore deregulation issues."

Oscar had no idea what that was. "What does that mean?"

"It means he offers advice to the president on rules that control drugs, for one thing. Deregulation means to remove some, or all, of those rules.

They scanned the film from beginning to end, then returned to the beginning and repeated the process. This time, Jim looked closely at each image. There was one where Bouvoir seemed to be holding something. He adjusted the machine, and the image was magnified.

Oscar saw that the congressman was holding a framed picture. A few more adjustments and the framed picture came into clear focus. It was a portrait of a young child. He had heavy black hair, and on his right cheekbone was a painful-looking scar about three inches long.

"This is unbelievable! There's no mistaking who this is, Oscar. It's an early picture of Christian Bouvoir, the congressman's adopted son. Oscar, I don't know how to thank you. I don't understand how you did it, but I know this . . . if it weren't for you, I would still be stumbling around looking for something I knew nothing about. My father and brother would have died in vain."

Congressman Arrested—Linked to Organized Crime
Son Under Investigation

July 4, 1951
Times Correspondent
Jerome Wolters

Congressman Julian Bouvoir was placed in custody early this morning as the Federal Bureau of Investigation coordinated simultaneous raids on his Washington, DC office and his private residence in an upscale neighborhood of Fairfax, Virginia.

A seventeen-year member of the House of Representatives, Bouvoir has gained a reputation as a solid family man and a staunch supporter of government deregulation.

Bouvoir moved into politics in the mid-thirties, upsetting the conservative incumbent in a close election. He was listed as one of the wealthiest congressmen in a 1940 survey. The majority of his fortune was made in the printing business during the late twenties and early thirties, but since that time, he has invested heavily in family entertainment enterprises.

The arrest was a surprise development and the result of an ongoing probe by the FBI. Accused of being a prominent member of organized crime, Bouvoir is suspected of being backed by drug money originating in both South America and the Far East.

In a related matter, his adopted son, Christian Bouvoir, is under investigation for illegal money laundering. *The Times* received an anonymous letter stating the younger Bouvoir was the son of the notorious Colombian drug boss, Carlos Arrabo.

Christian Bouvoir was planning a major foray into the entertainment business through the development of the world's largest amusement enterprise. The location of this proposed mega amusement park has not yet been divulged.

Epilogue

It was early April, and school was in session. Ten months had passed since Oscar received the Wild Ways. Larry was fully recovered from his sickness, and although separated in age by nearly two years, Oscar and Larry were in the same grade and had the same teacher. Mrs. Peterson was, they agreed, the best teacher in the school, and they were lucky to have her.

Mrs. Peterson appeared glad to have the two boys in her classroom. They seemed mature beyond their years and had a stabilizing influence on the other students in her sixth-grade class. They started a "Critter Club" with fellow classmates that caught on with the whole school. The club members picked a different animal every month to research and report on. Every member of the club was finding a new appreciation for nature, and each gained a new respect for the animals they learned about.

There was what his parents called a "moderate reward" for helping solve the murders. In truth, it was a bank account established in Oscar Johnson's name, into which Jim Brandt placed money each month to help pay for Oscar's future college costs.

During Jim's frequent visits, he campaigned tirelessly with Oscar's mother to allow Oscar to visit him in Washington. So far, she had not agreed.

Jim had confidence in Oscar's ability to "sense" certain things that might help solve old mysteries, finally convincing the family that their son was special and that his abilities should be shared.

After much hand wringing and tears, they established a special code to be used when Jim needed Oscar's help. If Agent Brandt called their house and said the words "Uncle Jim," it would mean Oscar was needed. So far, it had not happened, although Oscar expected it every time the phone rang.

"Is that Uncle Jim?"

"No, Oscar, it isn't."

His mother finally lost her patience, and Oscar was forced to stop asking the question every time someone else answered the phone.

Archie the gopher took up residence along the foundation of Oscar's house. He had become nearly obsessed with mind transfer with Oscar, to the point Oscar had to take matters into his own hands.

"Look here, Archie. I know you've got a lot to say, but you've got to cut it back a little. You're driving me nuts."

"Nuts? Where? I like nuts. Say, Oscar, how about sharing some of those nuts with me?"

"For crying out loud, Archie, I mean it's driving me crazy. All you want to do is talk. You need to back off a little so I can do my school work, and don't talk to me when I'm reading a book."

It didn't happen right away, but they finally worked through a few things, and the communicating leveled off to where they shared information about real life things that mattered. Oscar learned that Ring had lost a good deal of his vigor and was now tutoring his brother's boy on the earth's history and the mystery of the Wild Ways.

* * *